"L"
IS FOR
LOVE

"L"
IS FOR
LOVE

•

Dorothy P. O'Neill

LL
O'Neill

AVALON BOOKS
NEW YORK

Library of Congress Catalog Card Number: 99-90981
ISBN 0-8034-9386-X
Published by Thomas Bouregy & Co., Inc.
401 Lafayette Street, New York, NY 10003

PRINTED IN THE UNITED STATES OF AMERICA
ON ACID-FREE PAPER
BY HADDON CRAFTSMEN, BLOOMSBURG, PENNSYLVANIA

To my family of advisers:

Mary and Bill Barlow,
who helped me make the switch from typewriter to word
processor, and gave me a computer that does everything except
think up plots.

Dwight Barlow and Roger Barlow,
whose knowledge of auto mechanics kept me from making
technical blunders.

Dr. Bob Barlow,
who provided me with correct medical facts and terminology.

Thanks kids.

Chapter One

Tracey Wood drove her mother's 1987 Buick wagon down the hill into the Saturday afternoon traffic on Victory Boulevard. She and Mother called the old car the Blue Bomb. When it was new, Dad had named it the Blue Streak, but that name was history, along with her parents' marriage.

She hadn't driven it much during the two years since Dad had given her the Mercedes for her college graduation. Today Mother had asked to borrow the Mercedes.

"I'm picking up an out-of-town couple at the ferry and showing them a six-hundred-thousand-dollar home this afternoon." she'd explained.

Tracey needed no further explanation. The Mercedes was better suited to picking up prospective buyers of big-bucks houses than an aging wagon.

"No problem," she'd replied. "I'm only going over to Nita's this afternoon. I can take the Blue Bomb."

Why did Mother hang onto that old car? she wondered. There was no reason why she couldn't buy a new one. She could even buy a Mercedes of her own if she chose to. During the nine years since she and Dad divorced, she'd become one of the most successful real estate brokers on Staten Island.

Maybe driving the car Dad had given her for a long-ago wedding anniversary was Mother's way of clinging to the last vestige of happier days, Tracey thought, as she maneuvered the Buick into the left-hand lane. Or maybe keeping the old car was part of the bitterness so evident every time Mother spoke of Dad.

"I hope you told your father I'm still driving around in this old heap while he gets himself a new luxury model every year," she'd say. Then she'd follow up with "your father was too wrapped up in his big business deals to be a good husband and father."

Tracey had grown weary of reminding her that Dad's preoccupation with his business had provided them with a luxurious lifestyle before the divorce and that nothing much had changed since. He'd awarded Mother a generous settlement that included their spacious English Tudor style home on Grymes Hill and its furnishings—sterling silver, mahogany, Persian rugs and all. Besides that, the prestigious boarding school and college and the Mercedes proved he was anything but a deadbeat Dad.

Mother might be less bitter had she known why Dad wanted the divorce. She claimed she didn't know. One day he just told her he wanted out of the marriage and moved to his Manhattan club and then to the posh Park Avenue apartment where he still lived when he wasn't at his lodge in Maine or sailing his yacht around the Caribbean.

At first Mother thought there must be another woman. "A young woman, half his age, with an eye on his wallet," she'd say, but when he didn't remarry for nearly six years, and then to the fifty-something widow of a business colleague, she decided there had to be some other reason. "I wish I knew what it was," she often said.

Tracey was as much in the dark as she. It wasn't as if Mother had let herself go. She'd kept her pretty blonde looks and good figure. She was a college graduate and had been talking about going for her master's degree before the divorce, so it wasn't as if she wasn't Dad's mental equal.

When Tracey asked her father why he left, all he said was he was sorry and he'd explain someday, but the day never came. He told her he'd always be her father and he'd always love her and they'd see each other as much as possible.

Now, as she braked for a red light at the intersection of Victory Boulevard and Forest Avenue, she found herself recalling the years before the divorce. Mother and Dad had seemed happy. There'd been nothing to indicate an impending breakup. Their frequent arguments seemed more like teasing than serious disagreements. She remembered Mother calling Dad a twelfth-grade tycoon—whatever *that* meant.

Even though Dad's business had kept him away from home a good deal of the time, she missed him those first months after he left. But then she went away to boarding school, and after that there was college. She spent part of her vacation time with him and, to her surprise, she found herself seeing almost as much of him after the divorce as before. As for his new wife, she liked her, but she could never admit that to Mother.

Meanwhile, life with Mother was okay. They got along better than many mothers and daughters. Mother was good company, except when she started complaining about Dad. If only she wasn't so bitter, they'd both be happier, Tracey thought.

"Your father was making peanuts when we met," Mother would say during one of her bitter tirades. "I married him anyway, and stuck by him while he was struggling to get ahead. Well, he got ahead, all right, by putting his business ahead of his family."

Lately, she'd been adding some advice. "Just because your father left us doesn't mean I believe all men are alike. I want you to fall in love and get married to a man who puts family first. I don't want you to make the same mistake I did."

Tracey knew Mother was beginning to suspect the

divorce had left her skeptical about marriage. She liked men, but she shied away from romantic involvement. Although there had been several men in her life during college and since, they'd moved on when they discovered she wasn't interested in a serious commitment.

She thought of Larry, a man she'd been seeing for a few weeks. What she liked most about him was his staunch support of equality of the sexes. He'd told her it was time society recognized that women were not helpless creatures, designed to be patronized by men. She didn't mind when he alighted from his Porsche, leaving her to get out without assistance. This was part of an attitude she admired. She'd hoped Larry wouldn't want to get serious anytime soon.

The light turned green. She stepped on the accelerator and felt the Buick falter for an instant before the engine stalled, leaving her immobile on one of Staten Island's busiest streets. She attempted to restart it without success.

Luckily, traffic was light at the moment, but she knew it wouldn't be long before there'd be a lane of vehicles piled up behind her and she'd hear horns blowing and see irate faces glaring at her. As if she'd *chosen* to sit there at a green light, she thought, already annoyed and ready to glare back at the first honker.

She decided to turn on the emergency flashers and raise the hood and call Triple A on her cell phone. Not that she'd recognize the trouble under the hood, but it would help inform oncoming drivers that she wasn't deliberately blocking traffic. Good thing she'd worn an ankle-length denim dress instead of a T-shirt and shorts, she thought. She was in no mood to hear male whistles.

After lifting the hood, she reached into her purse for the phone when she heard a man's voice calling to her. "I'll be right with you."

A white Ford panel truck had pulled up behind the Blue Bomb. A moment later a tall young man wearing khaki shorts and a white sports shirt appeared. She had an instant's impression of dark eyes and a friendly smile before his head and shoulders were under the hood and all she could see of him were his shorts and a pair of long, muscular legs.

"This is so nice of you," she said. "I'm ashamed to say, I never learned anything about cars."

His reply came up from amid the maze of cables and cylinders. "Women shouldn't have to learn about fixing cars, especially pretty, blue-eyed blondes."

She felt herself bristling. This guy should know the era of the dumb blonde stereotype was long gone. What he meant as a compliment was a sexist remark.

"My college roommate knows how to change a tire and lots of other things, too," she retorted.

"Good for her," he replied. "Do they offer courses in auto mechanics at your college?" Without waiting for a reply, he withdrew from beneath the hood and spoke again. "I think it will be okay now. You want to give it a try?"

As she walked around to get behind the wheel, she noticed lettering on his truck. FERRONE'S AUTOMOTIVE SERVICE. No wonder he was able to find the trouble so quickly, she thought. He was a mechanic.

She hit the ignition key. The engine responded instantly.

He closed the hood and came to the car window. "The coil wire fell off, that's all," he said, brushing an unruly strand of dark brown hair away from his brow.

She took a good look at him, noticing how his smile gently crinkled his ruggedly-handsome face. She caught a whiff of spicy aftershave lotion. This must be his day off, or he wouldn't be freshly shaven and wearing a clean white shirt. And khaki shorts, too, she thought, recalling his long, muscular legs.

On a scale of one to ten for looks and grooming, he'd be a nine-plus, she decided. Not at all the grubby, overall-wearing stereotype of an auto mechanic. If it hadn't been for the lettering on the truck, she wouldn't have known. Yes, it was his day off, she decided, but why was he driving his boss's truck?

Suddenly she became aware of his dark eyes observing her. Did he realize she'd been staring at him?

"Thank you very much," she said. "How much do I owe you?"

He shook his head. "It was my pleasure to rescue a damsel in distress."

After his previous remark, this otherwise innocent statement made her seem too helpless. "I insist on paying you for your time and your expertise," she said.

He laughed. "My time? How long was it—five minutes?"

"It would have taken a lot longer if you didn't know what to look for."

"If you're referring to my expertise, there's no charge for that either."

She glanced over her shoulder at the truck. "Will I have to contact your boss at Ferrone's Automotive Service and ask him to send me a bill?"

"That won't be necessary," he said with a grin. "There's something I should tell you, but we'd better get out of this traffic. If you'll turn onto Forest Avenue and pull over onto the first side street, I'll follow you and explain."

What could he possibly have to explain? she wondered. "All right," she said.

A few minutes later she parked the wagon on a side street. He parked nearby.

As he strode toward her car, she rolled down the window. "What did you want to tell me?"

"About you asking my boss to send you a bill—" he began.

She interrupted him with a sigh of annoyance. "Are we back to that? I thought I made myself clear."

"You did," he replied, "but I'm my own boss, and I think I have the right to do someone a favor if I want to." He held out his hand. "I'm Nick Ferrone, owner of Ferrone's Automotive Service. I wasn't driving around looking for some pretty, helpless female to assist. We close the shop at noon on Saturdays. I was on my way home."

That didn't explain the fresh shave and clean clothes, she thought in the midst of her surprise. Taking his offered handshake, she said, "Oh." Even his "helpless female" remark failed to stir a more complete reply.

She saw him glance at her left hand and suspected a wedding ring check. Apparently pleased, he cast her a grin. "Have I made my point, Miss. . . . ?"

"Tracey Wood," she replied. "And, boss or not, Nick Ferrone, you did go out of your way to help me."

He laughed. "You drive a hard bargain, Tracey Wood. Tell you what. My favorite pizza place is only a couple of minutes from here. You can treat me to lunch. Will that settle it?"

She hesitated for a moment. She was on her way to Nita's house for lunch and girl-talk about Nita's forthcoming wedding. "Well, okay," she said. "I was going somewhere for lunch, but I'll phone and say I'll be there later."

"And I'll call my mother to let her know I won't be home for lunch," he said.

So, he lives with his mother, she thought, watching

him go back to his truck. Appearances were deceiving. He looked more like the type who'd have his own place.

Taking her first bite of pizza, she sighed in satisfaction. "Now I know why you wanted to come here. This is really good."

He nodded. "I come here a lot. It's close to home. I live near Silver Lake Park in the same house where I grew up."

So, he lived with his mother in his childhood home, she thought. "Do you have brothers or sisters at home?" she asked.

He laughed. "Would you believe, besides my parents and me, my three sisters and two grandparents and an aunt all live in the house. We're like that family on television. I guess you could call us the Italian Waltons."

She smiled at the comparison. "It must be great, having a big family. I'm an only child and my parents are divorced. All my grandparents have died, and the only relatives I have are some cousins in California, so it's just my mother and me. We live on Grymes Hill, about half a mile north of Wagner College."

"I know that area," he said. "Wagner's my alma mater."

"You went to Wagner? Maybe you knew my friend, Nita Harrigan."

"The name doesn't ring a bell," he said, "but if she's

as young as you are, I probably graduated before she ever got there."

"We're not as young as that. We've both been out of college for two years."

"I've been out for five," he said.

Tracey did a quick calculation. Many men his age were married and if they weren't, most didn't still live with their parents. They didn't have to call their mothers to say they wouldn't be home for lunch. Was Nick Ferrone a mama's boy?

"You mentioned a college roommate before," he said. "Where did you go?"

"Mt. Holyoke."

"Right up there with the Ivy League. I guess you didn't have any trouble landing a good job."

"I did get a great job," she said. "I'm in television program production. But I must admit, my father helped me land the job. He knows a lot of people."

"Television production! That's a big job for a woman."

Before she could think of an appropriate retort to his sexist remark, he spoke again.

"I had help from *my* father, too. He loaned me the money to start my business. I was surprised when he offered to do it. He wanted me to go to law school."

"Is your father an attorney?"

"Yes. I know he was disappointed I didn't want to follow in his footsteps, but I've been a motor-head since I was around twelve, and I guess he knew I wouldn't be happy in any other line of work."

"What does your mother do?"

"She was a teacher until the first kid came along. That was me. Since then she hasn't worked outside the home."

"Was that her idea or your father's?" Tracey asked.

A slight frown crossed his face. "Do you think my old man insisted she stay home to make meatballs and tend the bambinos?"

"Sorry, I didn't mean that the way it sounded," she said. But she knew she had. She'd decided his father was the head-of-the-house, what's-for-dinner type, and, judging from the sexist remarks she'd heard Nick Ferrone make, it was like father like son.

"What does *your* mother do?" he asked.

"She's in real estate."

"I think I've heard of her. Christine Wood?"

Tracey nodded. She sensed her remark about his father still rankled him, and she regretted having made it. Despite being a male chauvinist, he seemed like a nice guy. She had to admit she felt strongly attracted to him.

While pretending to concentrate on eating, she stole a long look at him. To her embarrassment, their glances met.

He smiled. "Excuse me for staring at you. You're nice to look at," he said.

She felt her heart flip. His smile, his ruggedly handsome face, his athletic physique and his sense of humor all added up to a powerful magnetism. And there was no mistaking the look in his eyes. She sensed if she didn't leave within the next few minutes, he'd ask her if she were seeing anyone special. She couldn't be sure of how she'd answer.

"Thanks for the compliment," she said, scooping up the check. "I must be on my way. My friend's expecting me."

She had no intentions of explaining the friend was Nita, the one who'd gone to Wagner, and that Nita was getting married in two weeks. Somehow she found herself telling him this and more. "It's going to be a small afternoon wedding at her church, and then there'll be a reception at the country club," she said. "Nita's my best friend. We have a lot to talk about."

"I know about wedding talk. My sister, Estelle, is getting married soon, too. Are you going to be a bridesmaid in your friend's wedding?"

Tracey shook her head. "Her sister is going to be her only attendant." She stood up. "Well, thanks again for your help with the car, Nick."

He got to his feet. "So long, Tracey. Thanks for the chow."

She turned away, quickly, from his smile, telling herself these unwanted feelings would go away once she was out of range. As an added defense, she reminded herself Nick Ferrone, for all his masculine magnetism, was a chavinist male and possibly a mama's boy as well.

Chapter Two

Nita lived with her parents in a neighborhood of tree-shaded streets and well-tended lawns. When Tracey turned the Blue Bomb into the driveway of the large, red-brick house, Nita came out the front door.

"What happened?" she called, as Tracey got out of the car. "Why couldn't you make it for lunch?"

"Mom's wagon broke down on Victory Boulevard," Tracey replied. "A man came along and fixed it. He wouldn't take any money, so I treated him to a pizza." As she spoke, Nick Ferrone's smile flashed into her mind. She felt herself on the brink of a blush.

Nita cast her a curious look. "Something tells me he wasn't old and paunchy," she said.

"Well, no, he wasn't," Tracey replied, following her into the house.

Nita laughed. "Okay," she said, settling herself in a living room chair. "Sit down and tell me all about it."

14

Moments later, her eyes widened and her eyebrows disappeared beneath her auburn bangs. "Nick Ferrone! I remember him from Wagner when I was a freshman and he was a senior. Of course he didn't know I existed. He was captain of the football team and president of the student council and absolutely the best-looking guy on campus. Did he tell you what he's been doing since college?"

"He owns an auto repair business."

Nita nodded. "That figures. Word around campus was he could fix anything on wheels. Is he married?"

"I don't think so. He told me he lives in his parents' house with his three sisters and a bunch of other relatives. He didn't mention a wife."

"Are you going to see him again?"

"Nita . . ." Tracey shook her head in exasperation. "Don't get any ideas."

"Why not? I can tell by the look in your eyes that you like him, and he must like you, too, or he wouldn't have wanted to go for pizza. I'll bet he phones you."

"Don't hold your breath. He didn't ask for my number."

The instant the words were spoken she realized Nick knew her name and her mother's name and where they lived. If he wanted to call her, it would be easy for him to find her number in the book. Suddenly she found herself hoping he'd call.

"How many Woods could there be in the phone

book with a Grymes Hill address?" Nita asked. "I hope
he calls you. You need some romantic excitement in
your life, Tracey."

"I don't need a romance with Nick Ferrone or anyone else," Tracey replied.

"I only want you to be as happy as I am," Nita
replied. "You don't know what you're missing, not
being in love with a wonderful man you know you're
going to spend the rest of your life with."

Mother had believed she was going to spend the rest
of her life with Dad, Tracey thought. "I'm content just
being friends with guys and avoiding the 'L' word,"
she said.

Nita shook her head. "Listen to yourself, you can't
even *say* love."

"Can we talk about something else?" Tracey asked.

"Sure we can. Have you asked Larry to escort you
to my wedding?"

"Would it be okay if I just came by myself?"

Nita frowned. "You know I expected you to ask
someone." Suddenly the frown vanished. She gave a
teasing smile. "Are you afraid the romantic atmosphere of a wedding might make you see Larry as
more than a friend?"

"It's the other way around," Tracey replied. "I don't
want Larry getting ideas. We have a nice, comfortable,
uncommitted relationship, and I want to keep it that
way."

Her life was exactly the way she wanted it, she thought. She had good friends and a great job with a future. She didn't need anything more.

Strong as these thoughts were, they failed to keep Nick Ferrone out of her mind.

"If you can't fall for a man like Larry, I'm afraid there's no hope for you," Nita said. "If I weren't madly in love with Don and about to be married, I could go for him myself."

Suddenly she bounced out of her chair. "Oh, I didn't tell you about the fantastic wedding present I got from my Aunt Louise. It's in the dining room."

Tracey followed her across the hallway. On the dining room buffet stood a mahogany silverware chest.

"Here it is," Nita said, lifting the lid. "Eight place settings of sterling silver."

"What a super gift," Tracey said, gazing at the gleaming array of knives, forks and spoons. "This silver will fit right into the romantic candlelight dinners you're going to fix for Don."

"Right," Nita said with a dreamy smile. "There's no dining room in the apartment, but our kitchen table will look like it's straight out of *House Beautiful*."

If Nick Ferrone ever got married, he'd take his bride home to live with his family so he could go on being near his mother, Tracey thought. She pictured them all gathered around a huge dining room table with Nick's mother serving his favorite foods, while Nick praised her cooking and his hapless wife cringed, knowing she'd never be able to cook like Mama.

When she returned home, she found Mother at her computer in the den.

"Good news, Tracey," she said. "I sold the big house."

"You're a wiz, Mom. Congratulations," Tracey said. She almost added, "maybe now you can think about getting a new car." Instead, she told her about the Blue Bomb breaking down on Victory Boulevard.

"Oh my," Mother said. "That could have ruined the sale for me if I'd had my clients in that car. Lucky I had your car. Thanks for letting me use it, dear."

Sometimes Tracey wished Dad hadn't given her the Mercedes. Having Mother thank her for the use of it made her feel guilty.

"What did you do, dear? Were you able to get Triple A?" Mother asked.

"I was just about to call them when a nice man came along," Tracey replied. "He located the problem and fixed it. A coil had come loose or fallen off or something. Nothing serious."

A nice man. This was a pallid description of Nick Ferrone, Tracey thought. With a frown, she realized her unwanted feelings had not diminished.

"Are you sure it wasn't something serious that could cause more trouble?" Mother asked.

"Fortunately, the man was an auto mechanic. He didn't think anything else would happen."

"That *was* fortunate. What did he charge? I'll pay you back.''

"He wouldn't take any money." As Tracey relayed the entire incident, thoughts of Nick's smile kept intruding. She felt her face grow warm with a blush. She hoped Mother didn't notice.

The phone on a nearby table rang.

"I'll get it," Tracey said. "That's probably Larry, letting me know what time he's picking me up tonight."

The voice responding to her "hello," however, did not belong to Larry.

"Tracey, this is Nick Ferrone. I'm calling to see if your car's running okay now."

She thought her voice sounded amazingly calm, even though she found herself short of breath. "Oh, Nick, thanks for calling. The car didn't give me any more trouble," she managed to say.

"I got thinking about it and thought maybe I should have another look at it, just to make sure it's okay," he said. "I could take a run up to your place tomorrow afternoon if that's convenient."

Now was her chance to put an end to this, she thought. She could say it wasn't convenient, or they'd have their regular mechanic look at it. "Tomorrow afternoon will be fine, Nick," she heard herself saying.

"Say, around three?" he asked.

"Three's good. Do you need directions?"

"No, thanks. I know my way around that neck of the woods. See you tomorrow, Tracey."

Mother looked at her in puzzlement. "Who's Nick?"

"He's the mechanic I treated to pizza after he rescued me today."

"And he's rescuing you again tomorrow afternoon at three?" Mother asked with a laugh. "What's going on?"

"Nothing," Tracey replied, trying to make her voice sound calm and casual. "He just wants to make sure everything's okay with the Blue Bomb."

"Well, you can be sure he'll expect to be paid this time," Mother said. Suddenly she frowned. "I have an appointment at half past two tomorrow. . . ."

"Take my car. I hadn't planned to use it tomorrow anyway."

A suspicious look came into Mother's eyes. "Oh, thanks, dear, but are you sure you want to spend Sunday afternoon watching a mechanic go over the Blue Bomb?" she asked. Without waiting for a reply, she added, "You haven't told me everything, have you?"

There was nothing to do but make light of the situation, Tracey decided. "I can't fool you, Mom," she said. "You guessed it. Nick's not only a good mechanic, he's a nice guy. I wouldn't mind having him for a friend."

"Another *friend*?" Mother shook her head. "When are you going to settle down? I can't help feeling you've developed a distrust of men because your father abandoned us. Haven't I told you, over and over, all men are not like him?"

Tracey hated it when Mother bad-mouthed Dad. Though the divorce had made her skeptical about marriage, she did not feel abandoned. She loved Dad and knew he must have had a good reason to leave. She only wished she knew what it was.

Mother's bitterness should have been gone by now. If she truly believed all men were not like Dad, she'd had plenty of chances to find someone else. Instead, she'd drawn apart from long-time friends and given up activities she'd enjoyed before the divorce. She didn't play golf anymore; she used the country club only for business purposes. She also gave up her bridge club and her church and hospital volunteer work.

The sound of the phone broke into these reflections. It was Larry.

"Tracey, I'm sorry, but I have to call off tonight's date," he said. "I just finished a round of golf with an important client, and I want to wine and dine him here at the club."

"That's okay, Larry, I understand," she replied.

"You're always a good sport, Tracey," he said, "How about making it tomorrow night instead?"

"I can't make it tomorrow. . . ." She wondered why she'd said that. Nick would be gone long before evening.

When she hung up the phone, Mother looked at her with a wry smile. "Let me guess. Larry has a business dinner again," she said.

Tracey knew what was on Mother's mind. Larry was a man to whom business came first—like Dad.

"Don't worry, Mom," she said. "My feelings for Larry are strictly platonic."

Unlike her feelings for Nick Ferrone, she thought. She hadn't tried hard enough to suppress them. Starting this minute, she must double her efforts. Every time she found herself thinking about his smile and his eyes and his long, muscular legs and his great sense of humor, she must remind herself of his patronizing attitude toward women. She must not forget he was probably a mama's boy, too.

This was only an infatuation, she told herself, and she must get it under control, for if her feelings were this strong today, what would they be after tomorrow?

Chapter Three

The next day was gray and drizzly. At ten minutes to three, Tracey posted herself at the living room window and watched for Nick's truck. Like a teenager expecting her first date, she thought. In a way it was the same. This was the first time she'd felt such anticipation.

When the truck turned into the drive, she glanced at her watch. Two minutes to three. Mama had trained him to be on time for appointments, she thought.

She watched him get out of the truck and sprint through the rain. The sight of him stirred up all of yesterday's feelings. Not that they needed stirring; she'd spent last evening and most of today trying to quell them.

The doorbell sounded. Her heart pounding, she went to answer it.

His smile seemed even more exciting then yesterday. "Hello, Tracey," he said, "Dr. Ferrone's making a house call. How's the patient?"

"Doing nicely since your treatment yesterday, doctor," she replied. She felt grateful for the banter. It gave her time to calm herself. "Shall we go out to the infirmary?" she asked.

She led him through the kitchen into the three-car garage.

"This is some big ward for just one patient," he said.

She couldn't think of another medically-related reply. "My mother's out with the other car," she said.

He raised the Blue Bomb's hood. "I'll take a good look at it," he said. "I don't want you buying pizza for any more men."

Did he know what his joking remark did to her heart? As she managed a laugh, she realized he thought the Buick was hers. "This is my mother's wagon," she explained. "A few years ago we started calling it the Blue Bomb because we expect it to blow up any day."

"I'll find out if that's likely to happen," he said. "I want to start her up. Do you have the key?"

"I'll go get it," she said.

When she returned, he was probing around under the hood. "Looks fine so far," he said. He opened the garage door and asked her to start the car and let it idle while he continued his observations.

He was earnest about this, she thought, somewhat surprised. She'd half-suspected he was using the old

Bomb as an excuse to see her again. With a sinking feeling, she wondered if she'd imagined that look in his eyes.

His voice came into her thoughts. "Your wagon's in good shape. How many miles does it have on it?"

"I don't know," she replied. "I drive it so seldom, I never noticed."

He laughed. "Men generally check the odometer when they get behind the wheel."

She felt the familiar twinge of annoyance. "Meaning, women don't?" she asked. "That's not one hundred percent true. I watch the mileage on my own car regularly."

He opened the door on the driver's side of the Buick, evidently too curious about the mileage to ask what kind of car she had and what the odometer said.

"Eighty-one thousand miles," he announced.

While Tracey tried to decide whether this was bad or good, he spoke again. "That's not much for a car this age. It's got many more miles to go before it quits."

"Now that we know everything's okay, how about a cold drink?" she asked.

"A soda would be great, thanks," he replied.

They took their glasses out onto the screened porch, which overlooked the flagstone terrace and swimming pool.

"You have a beautiful home, Tracey," he said, settling himself in a cushiony wicker chair.

"Thanks. We love this old place. We're glad we were able to go on living here after the divorce."

"That's a great pool. Do you swim much?"

"Almost every evening after work, from late spring till early fall. Weekends, too, of course. Too bad it's raining today; we could have a swim. Mother keeps extra trunks and suits in the pool house for guests." But there hadn't been many guests since Dad left, she thought.

"Will you give me a rain check?" he asked.

"Sure." Did he expect her to set up a definite date? she wondered. Feeling as uncertain as a fourteen-year-old, she covered with a change of subject. "Tell me about your shop," she said.

His eyes lit up with enthusiasm. "I should warn you—when I get talking about my shop, I get carried away. What do you want to know?"

"Well, for one thing, where is it located?"

"It's in the New Dorp area. I bought an old repair garage from a guy who was retiring. It was so shabby and greasy, I almost didn't buy it, but the location was good and the price was right. I had to do plenty of fixing up before I opened. I wanted it to be a different kind of auto repair shop."

"Different? How?"

"I wanted it to be a female-friendly shop—where women could bring their cars in and not feel confused and uncertain in a male domain."

More helpless female talk, Tracey thought. "I don't

think women feel intimidated like that any more," she said.

"Not young women like you, but many older women like my mother and grandmother still do," he replied. "When I decided to go into the auto service business, I noticed there were a lot of older women drivers. I figured a large percentage of them might be widows whose husbands always used to take the cars to be serviced. For the first time in their lives, those women have to be responsible for their cars. I thought if I could provide a clean, comfortable place for them to wait if they had to, along with courtesy and good service, they'd become regular customers."

Tracey thought of the many times Mother had complained of waiting for the Buick to be inspected or the tires rotated, while sitting in an untidy area on a ratty, plastic chair outside a men's rest room. Even the dealership where she took her Mercedes wasn't a whole lot better. She had to admit that Nick's idea made sense.

"So, did you install a nice, clean waiting room, and did the older women flock to you?" she asked.

He nodded. "Sometimes it looks like a meeting of my grandmother's garden club," he said with a laugh. "I bring in recent copies of my mother's and sisters' magazines, and there's a TV and complimentary coffee and a soft drink machine. I make sure the ladies' rest room is kept clean, too. A cleaning service takes care of both rest rooms, and the ladies' area gets extra attention."

Tracey stared at him in disbelief. This had to be his mother's influence, she decided. "I'm impressed," she said. "Is this waiting room restricted to women, or are men allowed in?"

He laughed. "Men can wait there if they want to. I didn't want to get hauled up on charges of sex discrimination."

Hearing about his female-friendly repair shop gave Tracey a different slant on Nick's attitude toward women. Maybe she'd misjudged him. Maybe he just wanted women to be more comfortable in what he viewed as a man's world. An instant later she had second thoughts. If he believed it was a man's world he had to be a full-fledged male chauvinist.

"Besides providing a comfortable waiting room for women, I set myself up in a nice office," he said. "I even have a private shower so I can wash up after work."

That explained why he'd been clean and freshly shaven yesterday, she thought. The private shower in the shop must have been his mother's idea, she decided. Mama didn't want him coming home and greasing up the bathroom. Suddenly, she recalled his spicy aftershave. She'd never encounter that scent again without thinking of him.

"I've talked enough about my work," he said. "Tell

me about yours. You mentioned you were a television program producer."

"I'm not exactly a producer yet," she said. "I'm on the production staff of a daytime program called 'Road of Life.' " You probably never heard of it. It's a soap opera."

"You're right, I'm not into soap operas. Sounds like an interesting job."

"It is. I really love what I do. The people I work with are great."

"I guess you know all the actors and actresses on the show."

"Yes. They're a nice bunch. One of them has become a close friend."

He put on an exaggerated scowl. "Not a handsome hero actor, I hope."

The hint that he'd be jealous made her heart quicken. He was kidding, of course, she told herself. Well, she could kid right back. "Don't worry, you don't have any competition," she said. "My friend is an actress."

"That's a relief," he said with a grin.

Suddenly she found herself wishing he wasn't kidding. This was no way to put a damper on her feelings. She diverted the talk to safer ground. "My friend is a gorgeous brunette named Bianca Morelli. She plays a sultry siren. It's only a small part, but she's good at it."

"My mother and aunt watch soap operas," he said.

"I'm going to tell them I know someone who knows the sultry siren on 'Lifetime Road.' "

"It's 'Road of Life,' " she said, laughing.

At that moment, footsteps sounded in the house.

"My mother's home," Tracey said. She turned and called, "Hi, Mom, we're out here."

A moment later Mother came out onto the porch, looking chic and pretty, as usual. Without waiting for Tracey to introduce her to Nick, she smiled and held out her hand. "You must be the man who helped Tracey with the car yesterday. I'm Christine Wood, Tracey's mother." When she chose, Mother could be all charm, Tracey thought.

Nick had sprung to his feet the instant she appeared. He clasped her hand and smiled in return. "Nick Ferrone here. How do you do, Mrs. Wood? It's a pleasure to meet you," he said.

If Mother wasn't dazzled by his smile, she must at least have noticed his good manners, Tracey thought. Being a mama's boy had its fringe benefits.

"Tracey told me you were coming to look at my Buick and make sure it's not going to break down again anytime soon," Mother said. "Thanks. And thanks for rescuing her yesterday. Did you find anything else wrong with my car?"

"Not a thing, Mrs. Wood. From the looks of it, your wagon will be on the road for a long time."

"That's comforting," Mother replied. "I've become

attached to the old heap. I don't want to part with it unless absolutely necessary."

Emotionally attached to it, Tracey thought. Deep in Mother's subconscious, the Blue Bomb was still the Blue Streak.

"Well, I have some papers to go over," Mother said. "I hope you'll stay awhile, Nick, so we can visit later." With a smile and a wave of her hand, she went into the house.

"Your mother's a charming lady," Nick said.

"Most of the time," Tracey replied.

In response to his puzzled look, she explained. "My parents' divorce wasn't her idea. She never got over feeling bitter toward Dad, and sometimes her bitterness takes over." She hadn't meant to tell him this. Something made her want to confide in him.

She knew what he was thinking. Why would a man want to divorce such an attractive woman? She'd been asking herself the same question for nine years.

"I never would have suspected she could be anything but pleasant," he said.

"She liked you, Nick."

He smiled. "That's good. Having a girl's mother like you is next best to having *her* like you." A moment later his face sobered. "Tracey, I hope I'm not out of line asking you this. Is there . . . I mean, are you seeing someone?"

She caught her breath. A simple "yes" would end this once and for all, but the word would not come out. Instead, she heard herself saying, "Nobody special."

His eyes sought hers. She found herself drawn into a deep gaze. Her heart went into a spin.

"Would you go out with me sometime?" he asked.

She managed a reply. "Sure, Nick."

"How about next Saturday night? We could have dinner and take in a movie."

"Sounds good," she said. Larry would be surprised when he phoned her to make a date for Saturday night and she told him she was busy. She thought of the dates he'd broken because of business deals. Larry wouldn't mind a last-minute cancellation, just as he assumed she wouldn't mind. It was part of his view on equality.

"I'll phone you in a couple of days to make sure you haven't changed your mind," Nick said.

"Why would I change my mind?"

"You might have second thoughts about going out to dinner in a mechanic's truck."

"If you believe that matters to me, you must think I'm a snob," she said.

He laughed. "Don't get mad. I was only kidding. I'll borrow my mother's car."

He glanced at his watch and rose from his chair. "I must get going. I promised my mother I'd be home early."

More evidence of his attachment to his mother, she thought, with a twinge of misgiving.

As they walked into the front hall, Mother came down the stairs. "Leaving so soon, Nick? You didn't let me know what I owe you for inspecting the Buick," she said. "Would you prefer to send me a bill?"

"You don't owe me anything, Mrs. Wood," he replied. He looked at Tracey with a playful grin. "The truth is, I used your car as an excuse to see Tracey again."

Tracey's heart flipped.

Mother laughed. "Well, now that you've accomplished that, can't you stay awhile?"

"I'd like to, but I must get home," Nick replied. "It's my grandfather's birthday and my mother's giving a family party for him."

"A family party for your grandfather. . . ." Mother's voice sounded wistful. "Will all his children and grandchildren be there?"

"Yes. Some are coming from New Jersey. We'll have a houseful."

"I hope your grandfather enjoys his party," Mother said. "Come and see us again soon, Nick."

He looked at Tracey as he replied, "Thanks, Mrs. Wood, I will."

They stood in the doorway and watched him drive off.

"What a nice young man," Mother said. She cast Tracey a quizzical glance. "Is there something going on between you two?"

"Well, we do have a date for next Saturday night." Tracey replied. Just saying it excited her.

Mother looked pleased. "I like him," she said. "Not every young man would tear himself away to attend his grandfather's birthday party."

Tracey knew where the conversation was headed. Mother had Nick pegged as a man to whom family came first. This was probably true, but for Nick, Tracey feared, family was spelled m-o-t-h-e-r.

Something close to panic seized her. What had she gotten herself into? Maybe it wasn't too late. Maybe her feelings for him would go away if she never saw him again. Saturday night would be the point of no return. She could break the date and tell him she wasn't interested in making another.

This thought sent stabs of pain into her heart. She knew she needed support. If she told Mother that Nick was a mama's boy, Mother might agree dating him would be asking for trouble. The matter of his male chauvinism was something else she could use to sway Mother.

"Mom, there's something you should know about Nick," she said. "He didn't tear himself away—his mother did. I strongly suspect he's a mama's boy."

She waited for Mother to say a relationship with a mama's boy was doomed from the start, to agree that she should end it with Nick before it went any further.

Instead, Mother shook her head. "His mother wanted him home in time for the family party and he was considerate enough to go along with her wishes. There's nothing wrong with a man being nice to his mother, Tracey. It doesn't mean—"

Tracey interrupted. "Nick's been out of college for more than five years. He must be at least twenty-seven and he still lives with his parents."

Mother cast her a cold stare. "So what if he does? When I was your age, if a young man worked in the vicinity of his home and had strong family ties, he didn't leave till he got married. So what if Nick's close to his mother? He struck me as the kind of man who'd never let his family down."

Tracey recognized the signs. Mother was on the brink of one of her bitter tirades. In an effort to head it off, she brought up Nick's sexism. "Mom, that's not all. Besides being a mama's boy, he has a patronizing attitude toward women. He's—"

But there was no diverting Mother when her bitterness took over.

"Tracey, you're coming up with all sorts of excuses to avoid getting closer to this young man. You have a distrust in men and your father's to blame for that, leaving us as he did. He was never close to his parents. If he had been, he would have had a sense of family and he wouldn't have left us," she began.

Tracey braced herself for the recriminations she'd heard over and over. "Your father was a rotten husband and father . . . his business meant more to him than we did . . . he believed money could be a substitute. . . ." It was as if, not knowing why Dad wanted a divorce, Mother had seized upon his devotion to his business as the reason.

There was nothing to do but let the tirade run its course. It was over in a few minutes, but Tracey knew the bitterness that provoked it would always lurk beneath the veneer of Mother's charming manner.

"Well, I hope you'll forget all that nonsense about Nick being a mama's boy just because he's still living with his parents," Mother said. "He's just being a good son."

Far from feeling let down by this lack of support, Tracey felt relieved. In her heart she knew she could never have broken the Saturday night date.

"Okay, Mom, if you say it's nonsense, maybe it is," she said.

Whether or not Mother was right, there was no denying the spark she and Nick had between them. It had set her heart ablaze. It had burned its way into her mind.

Mama's boy . . . Chauvinist male. Though doused again and again with these terms, the flame would not die.

She was only a few steps away from the ''L'' word.

Chapter Four

"Don't forget your umbrella, dear," Mother said, as Tracey prepared to leave for work the following morning. "And wear your raincoat. The weather report says heavy rain all day."

Tracey nodded in agreement. Though it was only a short walk to the ferry from where she parked her car, she'd be drenched without proper rain gear. "I watched a late news show last night and heard a big storm has hit the North Carolina coast," she repied. "Maybe we're getting the fringes of it."

She didn't usually watch late-night television, but last night, after she'd turned out her light, conflicting thoughts whirled around in her mind. The way Nick smiled, the way his eyes could draw her into a heart-spinning gaze, the sound of his voice when he spoke her name all became entangled with the question— was he or wasn't he a mama's boy? She found Nick's chauvinist attitude becoming less of a threat than his possible attachment to his mother.

Unable to get to sleep, she'd switched on her TV. The drone of voices and the patter of rain on her window finally lulled her.

As she drove along Victory Boulevard toward the ferry, she passed the spot where the Blue Bomb had bombed. More thoughts of Nick crowded her mind. She, who'd always been able to keep her appreciation of male physical and mental qualities strictly within the bounds of friendship, was in danger of losing her heart to a man she'd met only two days ago and seen only twice. And, as if that wasn't bad enough, she suspected he might have too great an attachment to his mother.

Though some mama's boys got married, they didn't want to leave their mothers, she found herself thinking. They took their brides home to live with her.

This line of thought set off shock waves. It was an alien invasion into her mind. Facing the "L" word had been bad enough. Now this.

By the time she reached her parking garage, she felt as though her heartstrings were tied in a knot. Dazed, she sloshed through the pelting rain to the ferry terminal and made the 8:10 boat with minutes to spare. Soon after she'd seated herself in her usual area, Nita arrived. They'd been meeting on the 8:10 boat ever since they'd both started working in Manhattan.

"Only one more week at work till after Don and I

get back from our honeymoon," she said. "Mother wanted me to take this week off, too, but I didn't want to waste so much vacation time on wedding preparations. We do have a lot of last-minute things to attend to, though, like the final fitting on my gown, for one thing. Did I tell you I'm wearing my sister's veil? It's supposed to bring good luck. And we have to decide on the flowers for the church, and. . . ."

Tracey was grateful for the chatter. Her mind had not yet recovered from the shock of thinking about marriage. But she wanted to tell Nita how Nick had come to the house on the pretext of checking on the Blue Bomb. She wanted to tell her about the Saturday night date. There'd be no harm in that, she decided. She wouldn't have to reveal what was happening to her heart.

She told Nita at the first pause in the chatter.

Nita gave a delighted squeal. "Didn't I tell you he'd phone you?" she asked. She cast Tracey a penetrating look. "You like him a lot, don't you?"

Tracey held back the urge to let it all out. "Sure, I like him," she replied. "He's a nice guy."

"Nice enough to escort you to my wedding?"

"You're determined not to have me manless for the big event, aren't you?"

"You'd have a lot more fun if you brought someone. We're having a dance band. Besides, your escort's been included in the head count."

Tracey felt besieged by conflicting feelings. Though

still shocked by that invasive thought, the idea of going to Nita's wedding with Nick suddenly appealed to her. She imagined dancing with him. He was probably a good dancer. His mother had probably taught him. She imagined him dancing with his mother. . . .

Nita's voice came into her musing. "What in the world were you thinking about just now? Your face went from happy to grim in a few seconds."

Tracey concocted a semi-lie. "First, I was thinking about your wedding, and then I glanced out the window and noticed it's still raining hard. It's a long walk from the subway to the studio. I'd treat myself to a taxi, but you know how it is with cabs on Manhattan on a rainy day."

Nita nodded. "When it rains, I know I'm lucky," she said. She worked in the Wall Street area, within walking distance of the ferry. In bad weather she hopped on a bus at the terminal and got off right in front of her building. "But if I had a glamorous job like yours, I wouldn't mind walking in rain or snow or anything else," she added.

"My job isn't all that glamorous," Tracey replied. "Most of the time it's just routine work."

"But you get to meet celebrities, and you know all those soap opera characters, especially your friend on 'Road of Life.' "

"You mean Bianca Morelli," Tracey replied. Suddenly she remembered she was having lunch with Bianca today.

"She sounds so glamorous," Nita said. "I'll bet she lives in a fancy Manhattan apartment house where a bunch of other celebrities live and she goes to all the famous in-places."

Tracey laughed. "Bianca's beautiful, all right, but she's not exactly a celebrity yet. She came to New York a year ago and still lives in the same small apartment with two other girls."

"She'll probably go to Hollywood and become a big star," Nita said. "Lots of soap opera actresses get into the movies. You said you were going to invite her to spend a weekend with you. When are you going to ask her? I'd love to meet a real live soap opera star."

"Bianca's weekends are very much filled at present. She's in the middle of a new romance." Tracey said. "I won't ask her today, but I promise, when she breaks off with this current man, I'll set something up."

"Sounds like she's fickle," Nita said.

"Maybe. Or maybe she's just looking for the right man. Anyway, I'll make sure you get to meet her next time she's between loves," Tracey replied.

After the boat docked and they'd gone their separate ways, Tracey thought again about asking Nick to escort her to Nita's wedding. She thought about it on the subway and during the long, wet walk across town to Rockefeller Center.

A disturbing question flashed into her mind. What if she asked him and he turned her down? Just because they'd made a date for Saturday night didn't mean he'd want to see her after that. The idea that she might have imagined the spark between them and the look in his eyes sent a painful barb into her heart.

As if Nick's sexist attitude, the mama's boy factor and the shocking marriage thoughts weren't enough to trouble her, now she had doubts about Nick's feelings for her.

Soon after she got to her desk, Dad's secretary phoned to confirm a lunch date they'd made the last time she'd seen him. Dad was in London, the secretary said, but he'd be back in time for lunch on Wednesday.

Lunch dates with Dad always made Tracey feel like a princess. She enjoyed being picked up by the limo and whisked away to meet him at his club or some luxurious restaurant. Anticipation, plus a busy morning work schedule, drove her troubling thoughts away for a while. It was almost lunchtime before they returned to plague her.

At noon, Bianca came to her office, fresh from a "Road of Life" shoot and looking like Sophia Loren forty years ago.

"Where are we eating?" she asked, and then added, "What's the matter? You look depressed."

"It's nothing, really," Tracey replied.

Bianca laughed. "If I didn't know you've insulated yourself from romantic involvement, I'd say you were having man trouble."

If anyone knew about man trouble, it was Bianca,

Tracey thought. She'd be the ideal person to confide in. "I'll tell you all about it at lunch," she said.

They went to a café in Rockefeller Center's underground area of shops and restaurants. As soon as they ordered, Tracey unburdened herself.

"There's this man I want to invite to a wedding, but I'm not sure how he feels about me. I thought I knew, but suddenly I'm having doubts."

"Are you telling me you actually met a man whose feelings about you matter to you?" Bianca asked. Without waiting for a reply, she added, "This I have to hear. Tell me everything."

As Tracey described Nick and the circumstances of their meeting, her heart quickened and she felt the warmth of a blush upon her face, which she tried to ignore. "I've only seen him twice. We haven't even had a real date yet, but he asked me to go out this Saturday night."

"He wouldn't have asked you out if he wasn't attracted to you," Bianca said. "Why are you having doubts? Go ahead, ask him to that wedding. The worst that could happen would be him turning you down."

The very thought of this filled Tracey's heart with pain.

Bianca scrutinized her for a moment. "You've fallen hard for this man, haven't you?"

Tracey stirred her coffee. "I guess so," she replied. It was strange to hear herself admit it in words instead of thoughts.

"So it's finally happened to you," Bianca said, with a laugh. "He must be something special. Besides being tall, dark and handsome and good with cars, what's he like?"

"Well, he's intelligent and he makes me laugh."

"That's it?" Bianca asked.

Tracey knew she was wondering about kisses. "*Bianca*, I told you I've only seen him twice," she said.

"Are you telling me you've got it bad for a man you've never even kissed?"

"I guess we were too busy talking to think about kissing," Tracey replied.

Bianca gave a hearty laugh. "I'll bet *he* was thinking about it the entire time. I'm surprised he didn't try."

There might have been a kiss if Mother hadn't come home, Tracey thought. She recalled how courteous he'd been, how he'd leapt to his feet the instant Mother appeared. "Nick has good manners," she heard herself saying.

"Good manners!" Bianca laughed again. "Next, you'll be saying he's good to his mother."

The words hit home. She decided to confide further in Bianca. "There's something else I'm concerned about," she began. After she let it out her concerns about Nick's mother, Bianca's first comment was a question. "Does this Nick by any chance have an Italian background?"

"Yes, he does. How did you know?"

"I recognize the scenario," Bianca replied. "It was played out in my own family. Italian mothers can be possesive of their sons, especially when they're widows like my mother."

"You mean, you have a brother who's. . . ." Tracey hesitated.

Bianca said it for her. "Yes, Michael's a mama's boy. I didn't think he'd ever marry, but he eloped with a girl he'd been dating since high school. I guess it was the only way he dared get married. Ma was fit to be tied. She even consulted our parish priest to see if the marriage could be annulled."

"How could it be annulled??"

"Ma thought it could be because the bride wasn't Catholic. Mixed marriages can be grounds for annulment, but it didn't work this time."

Most likely Nick's family was Catholic, Tracey thought. She was Presbyterian.

She was almost afraid to ask the next question. "Your brother and his wife—where do they live?"

"In my mother's house, where else?" Bianca replied. "Sandra still hopes they'll get their own place, but I know Michael feels so guilty about his marriage, he'll make it up to Ma by staying with her forever."

Tracey supressed a sigh. "I hope your mother eventually grew to like your brother's wife."

Bianca shook her head. "It's been almost two years and she still treats Sandra like an outsider. My wimpy brother puts up with it. I'm afraid it's going to wreck the marriage."

That's exactly what his mother wanted, Tracey thought.

"I'm not saying all Italian mothers are like Ma, but from what you told me it sounds like the same pattern," Bianca said. "It's not too late for you to get out of this gracefully, if you want to. You haven't even kissed your mama's boy yet."

As often as Tracey had used the term "mama's boy" herself, she resented hearing Bianca refer to Nick that way. *Nick couldn't possibly be as wimpy as her brother,* she thought. She should have just asked Bianca about taking Nick to Nita's wedding and let it go at that.

"Bianca, we've talked enough about me," she said. "How's your new romance going?" *Listening to Bianca rave about the current man in her life would be a welcome respite from the turmoil in my mind,* she thought.

"Good luck with your Italian Stallion," Bianca said after lunch, as they parted at the elevators.

Tracey reflected on the epithet. Italian Stallion was more descriptive of Nick than Mama's Boy, but might it not also describe a man who'd lead a woman to think his feelings went deeper than they actually did?

Back at her desk, her thoughts grew even more troubled, with doubts about Nick's feelings for her looming large.

With a sigh, she recalled how carefree she used to be. If the Blue Bomb hadn't broken down, these thoughts would never have entered her mind. There'd be no doubt, confusion or turmoil.

And no Nick either.

She pondered on this. If she'd imagined the spark between them, if the look in his eyes was only an illusion, if she never saw him again after Saturday night, she knew she'd always be thankful their paths had crossed. He'd brought something into her life she'd never known before and might never know again.

Suddenly she understood why Mother clung to the Blue Bomb.

Chapter Five

Dark clouds and lashing rain greeted Tracey when she left the studios that evening. The storm had intensified since morning. Windblown and soggy and thankful to be home, she drove the Mercedes into the sanctuary of the garage.

Mother met her at the kitchen door with a smile of relief. "I'm glad you're home safe," she said. "I've been watching the weather channel. They're calling this a freak storm. It's going to get very bad, they say. It got so dark, I had to turn the lamps on. Was it rough coming over on the ferry?"

"At no time were we in danger of capsizing," Tracey replied with a laugh. "The worst part was walking those blocks to the subway and then from the ferry to the parking garage."

"I can see you're soaked," Mother said. "You'd better take a hot shower and get into dry clothes before you get chilled. You need a cup of tea to warm you up. I'll have it ready for you."

Mother could be a dear when she wanted to, Tracey thought as she went upstairs. At times like this, she was thankful she hadn't moved into her own place. She'd considered it more than once, but the thought of leaving Mother alone with her bitterness kept her from doing it.

When she came down in sweatpants, old sneakers and warm socks, she found a teapot and cups on a table in the den and logs ablaze in the fireplace, and she thought of bygone times when she and Mother and Dad would gather round the hearth. In her younger days there'd been marshmallows. Those times had grown fewer as Dad's burgeoning business took him away from home, until they didn't happen anymore.

After the divorce, the fireplace wasn't used much. Mother stopped ordering their annual supply of wood. The logs burning tonight were left over from the once-high woodpile in the garage. Open fires made a terrible mess, Mother said, and they were too much trouble.

"This is nice, Mom," Tracey said, curling up on the couch.

"I thought it would take away some of the dampness," Mother said, pouring the tea. She glanced toward the rain-pelted window. "Listen to that howling wind."

"Let's get the weather channel on and find out how long this is going to last," Tracey replied.

A meteorologist reported worsening weather. Again, the term "freak storm" was used.

"It can get as freaky as it likes," Mother said. "We're nice and cozy here by the fire."

They were into their second cup of tea when Mother remarked that it was time they cooked dinner. Just as she spoke they heard an ear-splitting noise, something like a loud crack of thunder. Seconds later the television and lamps went out.

Tracey made her way through the semi-darkness to the window. Outside, she could see the outlines of a fallen tree. One of the huge, old oaks along the street had crashed onto their grounds. *The same gust of wind that felled it must have knocked out the electric power,* she thought.

Mother joined her at the window. "It looks like that big tree near the driveway," she said. "I guess electricity's off all over the house, but I'll check the kitchen anyway. If the stove's out, we'll have to make do with sandwiches for dinner."

Tracey peered out into the rain-shrouded gloom. Dinner was her least concern. The sight of other trees writhing in the gale told her there could be more uprootings. She was especially worried about the venerable fir a few yards away from the den window.

Mother came back from the kitchen, saying it was totally out of commission. "I'll make tuna fish sandwiches," she said. "Have you seen the flashlight? The kitchen's quite dark."

Tracey found the flashlight in a desk drawer.

Mother went back to the kitchen, saying, "While I make the sandwiches, see if you can find our battery-powered radio. If this storm is as bad as they say, there'll be more about it on the news."

Tracey rummaged through the den cabinets in search of the radio. When she found it, she discovered it needed new batteries. She found some and inserted them. The radio came on.

Mother entered the room with the sandwiches just in time to catch a weather report. The storm was the worst to hit the Atlantic coast in more than a decade.

"Staten Island is bearing the brunt of it," the commentator said. "Abnormally high surf is battering the beaches. Low-lying areas are flooded, and in higher elevations gale-force winds are wreaking havoc with power lines."

He went on to say the Grymes Hill area of the island was being hit especially hard. Reports had come in about roads blocked by fallen trees and electric and phone lines downed.

"I hope this is over soon," Mother said. Just as she spoke, a bulletin came on. The gale blowing up from the Carolinas was on a collision course with a northeaster. The two storms were expected to collide off Staten Island within the next two hours. Grymes Hill residents were warned to remain indoors and take shelter in basements where possible.

"Next, they'll be issuing tornado warnings," Mother

said. "I suppose we should go down to the basement, just to be on the safe side." Though she spoke calmly, her face had gone pale.

"Don't worry," Tracey replied. "There's been no mention of tornadoes. Anyway, this house is solid as a rock." As she spoke, she thought of the huge, old fir tree outside the den. It was heavy enough to damage the house if it crashed down. "Let's take the sandwiches and the radio down to the basement," she said. "And candles. We can have a candlelight dinner in the laundry room."

She spoke lightly, trying to calm her own nerves, brushing away imageries of the old tree falling on the house, shattering windows, perhaps damaging the roof. Though she knew they'd be safe in the basement, she found herself trembling from a sense of isolation. Their closest neighbors' houses on either side stood beyond wide, shrubbed grounds. Others were across a road filled with rushing water and debris. She longed for the sound of a reassuring voice.

"As soon as this blows over, the neighbors will come around to see if we're okay," she said, as they went down the basement stairs. "Maybe we should have a storm party while we're all trapped up here on the hill." The joking remark was as much for her own spirits as for Mother's.

Knowing the phone lines were down brought on an extra sense of isolation. She thought of the southerly gale and the northeaster colliding. Meteorologists weren't kidding when they called this a freak storm, she thought. All they could do was wait it out.

Huddled on an old sofa in the laundry room, they nibbled at the sandwiches. They were both too nervous to eat much.

An hour passed. The roar of the storm penetrated the basement with no letup.

"This is one of those situations when it would help to have a man around," Mother said. "Not that your father would be around tonight even if he hadn't left us. He'd be in Hong Kong or Buenos Aires, wrapping up some big business deal."

Tracey tried to ignore the remark about Dad. But she had to agree, a male presence at this time would be comforting.

She thought of Nick. He must have heard about the devastation on Grymes Hill. Did he care enough about her to be concerned? Suddenly, she wanted to see him, to be warmed by his smile and the look in his eyes. She could only imagine the feel of his arms around her, but she knew she wanted that, too.

"You look pensive, dear," Mother said. "What are you thinking about?"

"I was wishing we weren't alone," Tracey replied. It was true. Her feeling of isolation had crystallized into an intense need for Nick. Again, she wondered if he might be thinking about her during the storm and if he cared enough about her to be concerned.

"I'm surprised Larry hasn't called to see how we're

doing," Mother said. "He has a cell phone and he knows your cell phone number, doesn't he?"

Tracey nodded. "Yes, he knows it." It didn't surprise her that Larry hadn't phoned. She didn't expect him to. That would be like saying women needed looking after—a breach of his stand on equality.

Nick didn't have her cell phone number. If he did, would he care enough to call?

"Listen," Mother said, suddenly. "Do you hear something upstairs?"

Above the noise of the storm, Tracey heard pounding. For an instant she thought it might be the big fir tree uprooted and falling against the house. But the sound was too regular—like someone knocking on a door.

"I think someone's at the front door," she said. "I'll go and see who it is." She started up the stairs.

"It might be one of the neighbors," Mother called after her. "Whoever it is shouldn't have come out in this storm."

Knowing someone was concerned about them eased Tracey's feeling of isolation for a few moments, but as she walked through the kitchen into the front hall, the feeling returned. But suddenly she knew it wasn't a sense of isolation she was feeling, but an intense need to see Nick.

She opened the door, ready to greet whatever kindly neighbor might have come to check on them. Through the drenching darkness she could barely see the outlines of someone standing there. She caught her breath. There was no denying her instincts. All of her senses told her it was Nick.

His voice came out of the shadows. "Hello, Tracey. I just happened to be in the neighborhood."

She wanted to throw her arms around him, to have him hold her close, to tell him how much his being here meant to her. Instead, she laughed and took his hand and brought him into the house, saying the storm hadn't affected his sense of humor.

Rivulets of water coursed off his hat onto his raincoat and dripped on the floor. "I'm sorry," he said, looking down at the puddles.

"You're *sorry?*" She laughed again. "You came all the way up here in this storm to check on us, and you're apologizing for bringing in a little water?"

In a daze of happiness, she helped him off with his rain gear. "How did you get up the hill?" she asked. "We heard the roads were blocked with fallen trees."

"The roads are still blocked," he replied. "I drove up the hill as far as I could, until I came to a big tree across the road. I left the truck there and walked the rest of the way."

"Oh, Nick, you took an awful chance. There are so many trees along these roads. You could have been hit by a falling branch, or even a whole tree."

"I had to come," he said. "When I heard Grymes Hill was in bad shape, I was worried about you and your mother, Tracey."

Those few words dispelled all her doubts about his feelings for her. Her heart sang.

"Is your mother okay?" he asked.

"Yes. She's in the basement. We're using the laundry room as our cyclone cellar. Let's go down. We can hang your wet things down there."

Mother looked at Nick in surprise. "How in the world did *you* get here?" she asked. Without waiting for him to tell her, she added, "Where are my manners? It doesn't matter how you got here. What matters is you were thoughtful enough to come."

"He walked most of the way up," Tracey said. "He heard the news broadcast about Grymes Hill." Every word she spoke was an affirmation of his feelings for her.

"You made your way through this terrible storm to check on us?" Mother asked. "Nick, I can't thank you enough. We've both been nervous and frightened. Only a few minutes ago I told Tracey I wished we had a man around."

"Well, you've got one now," Nick said. He glanced at Tracey as he spoke. Her heart went into a double flip.

Mother plumped up a cushion on the old sofa. "Sit down, Nick. You must be exhausted and chilled to the bone. Tracey, there's an afghan around here somewhere. And your feet are soaked, Nick. Take off your shoes and socks. Tracey, I think there are towels in the dryer. . . ."

"Mrs. Wood, you sound like my mother," he said with a grin.

A few minutes later he'd settled himself on the sofa with the afghan tucked around him and his bare feet swathed in a towel.

"With the electricity out, we can't make coffee for you," Mother said. "And all we can offer you to eat are tuna fish sandwiches."

"Thanks, but I'm okay, Mrs. Wood," he replied. "I ate dinner before I left the house. The power didn't go out in our area and my mother was able to cook."

"What did your . . . family think when you said you were going out on a night like this?" Tracey asked.

"They thought I was crazy, especially when I told them I was headed to check on some friends on Grymes Hill." He reached into his pocket and took out his phone. "I promised my mother I'd call and let her know I got here all right."

"You should spend the night here, Nick," Mother said. "There's talk of two storms colliding. I'm afraid it's going to get worse before it gets better."

Tracey's heart, already drumming, skipped a beat. Would he say he'd stay or would he have to ask his mother's permission when he phoned her?

"Thanks, Mrs. Wood, I'd like to take you up on that if it wouldn't be too much trouble," he replied.

"No trouble," Mother said. "The weather report said it's not safe to stay upstairs, but you can sleep on this couch and there are two old camping cots for Tracey and me. We can't offer you a luxurious bathroom but there are facilities down here."

"All the comforts of home," Nick said. "Thanks, Mrs. Wood."

He called his mother. "I got here okay," he said. "Yes, my friends are all right. . . . The storm's still going strong so they've asked me stay overnight. . . .I'll see you tomorrow, Mother . . . No, I don't know what time. . . ."

Tracey pictured his mother questioning him, perhaps suspecting he hadn't been altogether truthful about his "friends" on devastated Grymes Hill. *He'll get the third degree when he goes home tomorrow,* she thought.

At that moment, another weather bulletin came over the radio. The two storms were expected to collide at any moment. Grymes Hill residents were warned, again, to go to their basements.

Tracey looked into Nick's eyes. "I'm glad you're here."

"So am I," he replied.

"That makes three of us," Mother said. "At least there's one man who cares about what happens to us."

This is a veiled reference to Dad and Larry, Tracey thought. Larry, who could have phoned, deserved the remark, but Dad . . . "Mom, Dad's in London," she said. "He doesn't know about the storm."

Just then, a loud, frightening crash sounded from

above. The house seemed to shudder. Mother screamed.

"Take it easy, Mrs. Wood. I'll go up and see what happened," Nick said.

"There's a huge old fir tree near the den window," Tracey said. "I think it must have fallen and crashed into the house."

Nick was already on his way up the stairs, warning them to stay below.

Mother watched him go. "Tracey," she said, "I hope there's one excuse you're not going to make anymore."

Tracey looked at her in puzzlement. "What do you mean, Mom?"

"You've been making excuses for not developing a closer relationship with Nick. One of them was that he has a patronizing attitude toward women," Mother replied. "Well, if he has, I'm very thankful for it tonight."

Tracey pictured Nick abandoning his truck on a blocked road, making his way through howling wind and lashing rain, clambering over fallen trees and dodging flying debris, because he knew two women were alone and frightened.

"I'm thankful for it, too, Mom," she said.

Mother smiled, "Then, can we strike that one off the list?"

Tracey thought of Larry, self-proclaimed champion of equality for women. Once, she'd admired his attitude that women could take care of themselves. Now she knew he'd never understand. No matter how independent a woman might consider herself, there were times when she needed the comfort of a man.

She nodded. "It isn't important anymore."

"Good," Mother said. "Now, about that other one . . ."

The sound of Nick's footsteps on the stairs kept Tracey from answering. Mother wouldn't have liked her answer anyway. She couldn't as easily dismiss the matter of his attachment to his mother. How could the alien thought of marriage ever have stolen past this problem and into her mind?

"You're right, Tracey, the fir tree has crashed through a window in one of your downstairs rooms," Nick said. "I took a look upstairs, too. Your roof's okay. The tree grazed a bedroom window but the glass isn't broken."

"I'm thankful you're here, Nick," Tracey said. The words sounded flat compared to her thoughts. She felt overwhelmed by the longing to be in his arms.

"Thanks so much, Nick," Mother said. "I'm glad there wasn't more damage."

"If you have anything like a tarpaulin, I'll rig something up to make sure your house stays dry," Nick said.

Tracey looked around and found something suitable. Nick took it upstairs to attend to the window. While he was there, she and Mother rummaged around the basement and found the camping cots and old sheets and blankets. They hadn't been used since their last camping trip with Dad. *That was the summer before he got too busy for family outings,* Tracey recalled. She was surprised Mother hadn't thrown the camping stuff away. Maybe she kept everything because it represented happier days. Like the Blue Bomb.

They had the cots set up by the time Nick came back to the basement. He grinned when he saw them.

"This is like Boy Scout camp, except we didn't have pretty blondes in our tents," he said.

Though he hadn't said "helpless blondes," I might have resented the remark not so long ago, Tracey thought. What a chip she'd borne on her shoulder!

They listened to another weather report. The meteorologist announced the two storms, now combined, were stalled over Staten Island. Again, Grymes Hill residents were warned to remain in their basements.

"We might as well talk until the next report comes on," Mother said. "It's too early for the bugler."

"What bugler?" Tracey and Nick asked in unison.

"Why, the one who blows taps, of course," Mother replied.

As they all laughed, Tracey could not help feeling some regret. Mother could be fun. She had so much to offer, but she'd allowed her bitterness to drag her away from the life she should be enjoying. She'd withdrawn from everything except her real estate career.

"Tell us about your family, Nick," Mother said. "Tracey says you have three sisters. Are you the only son?"

Tracey saw where this was going. Mother had made up her mind to get "mama's boy" crossed off the list, too.

"Yes," Nick replied. "If it weren't for my father and grandfather, I'd be surrounded by women. My three sisters, my mother, my aunt and my grandmother— that's a lot of females."

"With all those women around, I guess your mother gets plenty of help running the house," Mother said.

What was she driving at? Tracey wondered.

"Not as much help as she needs," Nick replied. "Two of my sisters have demanding jobs. The youngest one's still in college and Aunt Tessie's not in the best of health. My grandmother pitches in, though. If it weren't for her, it would be too much."

"Your mother sounds like a wonderful woman," Mother said.

Was she trying to have Nick's mother come across as some kind of saint? Tracey wondered. *Did she think this would change anything?*

"Tell Mom about your shop, Nick," she said.

Nick described his female-friendly automotive service. While Mother was telling him what a good idea it was, another weather bulletin came over the radio. The storm showed no sign of letting up. Again, hill residents were warned to remain in their basements.

They went to bed soon afterwards.

With Nick on the sofa, only a few feet away, Tracey expected she'd have trouble sleeping. Hearing his breathing, picturing his stalwart form stretched out under the old afghan, would surely keep her awake half the night, she thought. And, unaccustomed to sleeping in her clothes, she'd toss and turn, listening to the storm, thinking about Bianca's brother, telling herself her feelings for Nick must not progress beyond this point.

To her surprise, she felt drowsy almost immediately. It was as though Nick's presence had calmed the turmoil in her mind. Come what may, she knew their hearts were in sync. For now, this was all she needed.

Tomorrow, she'd ask him to escort her to Nita's wedding.

Chapter Six

W hen Tracey wakened the next morning, she looked across the room at the old sofa. Nick was not there, and his shoes and socks were missing from the laundry rack where he'd put them to dry last night. The sound of footsteps overhead told her he'd gone upstairs.

Mother was still sound asleep. She glanced at her watch. It was ten minutes to six.

She went to the basement lavatory. When she looked at her reflection in the mirror above the sink, she groaned. Nick wouldn't say she was good to look at this morning, she thought, as she ran a hand through her uncombed hair.

She stole up the basement stairs. She wanted to go up to her bedroom and make herself more presentable before Nick saw her, but when she stepped into the kitchen, she found him at the sink, drawing water into a long-handled pot.

"Good morning," she said, smoothing her hair.

He turned away from the sink and smiled into her eyes. "Good morning to you, too, Tracey." He gestured toward the window. "The storm passed during the night. It's stopped raining. I went outside to look around. The only real damage to your house is that broken window. I ran into one of your neighbors and he told me part of his roof had blown off."

"We're lucky to have a slate roof."

"That's what your neighbor said. Incidentally, I could tell he was curious about me—who I am and how come I'm prowling around your place so early in the morning. I told him I'm a friend of the family."

He was that and more, she thought. He'd won Mother over completely. As for herself, she could not deny he'd taken her another step closer to the "L" word.

"We'll never forget what you did for us," she said. "I hope you managed to get some sleep on that old couch."

"Sure I did, and you look as if you slept well, too." He cast her a teasing grin. "You look cute with your hair tousled."

"Thanks, I needed that," she replied.

He ran his hand over his beard-stubbled chin. "Aren't you going to tell me I look cute, too?"

"No, but I do like to see a man in the kitchen with a cooking pot. What are you doing with it?"

"The power's still off, so I got the fireplace going and I'm going to boil some water for coffee. I noticed you have some of those little coffee bags."

She must have looked doubtful. He laughed and explained. "When I was outside I found this," he said, lifting up an old iron plant stand. "The pot fits in it, and it's just the right height to set on the fire."

"You're the ideal person to have around during a power outage," she said. "Mother will be delighted. She always says she's not human until she has her morning coffee." How could she indulge in this chit-chat while longing to feel his arms around her?

"Is your mother awake yet?" he asked.

"She was still sleeping when I came upstairs."

"Let's get the coffee going and take a mug down to her," he said.

She put a china coffee service, coffee bags and three mugs on a tray and took them into the den.

"I would never have thought of that," she said, watching him place the improvised pot stand on the fire. "When Dad used to take us camping, we always had a portable grill." *It's a wonder Mother hadn't hung onto that, too,* she thought.

"Did you go camping a lot with your dad?" he asked.

"Yes. We used to go to different places—all over New England, the North Carolina Outer Banks, and one summer we went to Yellowstone Park. I missed those trips when Dad got too busy for vacations."

"Sounds like you had a good family life before your parents were divorced."

"We did." Suddenly she wanted to confide in him, to tell him neither she nor Mother knew why Dad wanted out of the marriage. She'd never told anyone about this, not even Nita.

"When my father left, it was a shocking surprise, especially to Mother," she said. "She still doesn't know why he wanted a divorce. Neither do I. There was no indication that they weren't getting along well. He was away on business a lot during the last couple of years of the marriage, but when he was home, everything seemed all right. And then, like a bolt from the blue. . . ." She shook her head. "When I asked Dad why, he said he'd tell me someday, but he never did, and I never asked him again."

She felt strangely enlightened, relieved to unburden the puzzlement she'd held in her heart for nine years.

"You were close to your father, weren't you?" he asked. "Do you see much of him now?"

"Oh, yes. Every week or so we have lunch or dinner, and I spend part of my vacations with him."

"Why don't you ask him why he wanted to end the marriage, Tracey? I can tell it's still bothering you, not knowing."

"I've thought about it, but after all this time it seems pointless."

"If he knew you'd carry this around with you all these years, he'd have told you."

"But if I asked him about it now, wouldn't that be digging up something buried long ago?"

He shook his head. "No, it wouldn't be digging something up, because you never buried it. Ask him, Tracey." As if to encourage her further, he patted her on the shoulder.

Like the look in his eyes, his touch generated vibes of excitement. She recalled what Bianca had said. *"You've fallen hard for a man you've never even kissed."* But she knew she didn't have to kiss Nick to find out how she felt about him. Knowing how much she wanted to was proof enough.

Nick's voice came into her thoughts. "Water's boiling."

Mother stirred and opened her eyes. "You're up. What time is it?" she asked, her voice still fogged with sleep.

"Coffee time," Nick replied, setting the tray on top of the washing machine.

"The power's still off, but Nick used the fireplace," Tracey added.

Mother sat up, smiling. "Coffee! Doing without it this morning would have been the worst part of the storm for me. Nick, you're a darling."

Tracey poured them each a mugful. Nick turned on the radio. He and Tracey sat down on the cot next to

Mother's. While they drank coffee and talked, they listened for a weather report. When it came on, they learned the twin storms, stalled for hours off Staten Island, had blown out to sea around midnight. Though Grymes Hill had been hit harder than anyplace in the New York area, sections of the island went almost unscathed, as did most of Manhattan and other boroughs. Staten Island's borough president announced that roads on Grymes Hill would be cleared by afternoon and power restored.

"That's good news," Mother said.

"Evidently it's business as usual in Manhattan," Tracey said. "I wish I could get in to work. I have an important meeting this morning."

"If you're up for walking to where I left the truck, I'll take you to the ferry," Nick said.

"Great," she replied. She glanced at her watch. "I have plenty of time to shower and dress in order to make the 8:10."

"Nick, if you want to take a shower, you can use the guest bath," Mother said. "Tracey will show you where it is. We keep a supply of toothbrushes and dentifrices there, but I'm sorry there's no razor or shaving cream."

"Thanks, Mrs. Wood, I'll take you up on that," Nick replied. "My shave can wait till I get home."

"You'll be okay alone, Mom, won't you?" Tracey asked.

Mother nodded. "I'll be fine. The power will come

on again soon and the roads will be cleared. I'll pick you up at the ferry tonight."

"Thanks, Mom. I'll phone you to let you know which boat I'm taking."

Tracey had never imagined that slogging through mud and debris would be at all enjoyable, but with Nick guiding her through puddles and helping her over fallen branches, it was almost romantic. Her heart leapt every time she felt his hand on her arm or their fingers entwined.

"Good thing you wore those heavy shoes," he said as they skirted a pool of muddy water.

She'd put on an old pair of hiking shoes and carried her others in a tote bag. She hadn't made any other concessions to the storm. With most of the metropolitan area not seriously affected, she didn't want to be the only one at work dressed like a refugee from a disaster area.

"It's hard to believe the storm concentrated on parts of Staten Island and barely touched the rest of the city," she said. "I hope your shop wasn't damaged."

"It's okay," he replied. "While I was in your guest room, one of my mechanics called me on my cell phone. He lives near the shop and he said he'd gone over there late last night to check and found everything all right." As he took her hand to help her through a mass of rubble, he added, "Thanks for being concerned, Tracey."

"I know how much your female-friendly shop means to you," she replied.

Though they got through the morass of twigs, stones and mud in a few seconds, he kept her hand with his. She thought he must surely feel her pulse racing.

They came to a large tree fallen across the road. Tracey saw Nick's truck on the other side of it.

"Looks like it's okay," he said, helping her clamber over the tree trunk.

Except for twigs on the roof and leaves plastered against the windshield, the truck was, indeed, none the worse for its night out in the storm. In a few minutes they were on their way to the ferry terminal.

"I want you to have my cell phone number and I'd like to have yours," he said, as they drove down Victory Boulevard.

It was only a simple request, Tracey thought, but the exchange of cell phone numbers suddenly became as romantic as an exchange of feelings spoken from the heart.

"Okay," she said. She took down his number in the small address book she carried in her purse, then wrote hers and handed it to him.

"We should have done this before," he said.

"Yes, we should have, but we really don't have much of a 'before,' do we?"

"It seems like we do," he replied.

It did, she thought. Was it only the day before yesterday that the Blue Bomb had stalled on Victory Boulevard?

"If you'd had my cell number before, you would have phoned me instead of braving the storm," she said.

He cast her a sidelong grin. "Don't be too sure about that."

It was difficult to go on bantering with her heart beating in triple time. She took a deep breath. "Well, anyway, I'm glad you showed up on our doorstep when you did. It meant a lot to Mother, too. You made her feel secure. Besides, I could tell she enjoyed having you stay overnight. It's been a long time since we've had guests. You drew her out of her shell."

He looked surprised. "You mean, she's been withdrawn since the divorce? I never would have guessed."

"She likes you, Nick. You're a good influence on her."

He laughed. "If I am, I'll have to make sure the influence continues."

She wanted to come back with a clever retort, something like his being a good influence on *her*, too, but she couldn't gather the right words. It was as if the time for banter had passed and anything she said to him now would be in earnest.

They reached the ferry terminal. He braked the truck at the passenger drop-off area.

"Thanks for the lift," she said. "And thanks again for checking on us last night."

"So long, Tracey. I'll call you before Saturday," he said with the smile that never failed to send her heart into a tailspin.

On the boat, during the few minutes before Nita arrived, she realized she hadn't asked him to go to Nita's wedding. She'd ask him Saturday night, she decided. If he said he couldn't make it, she knew it wouldn't have anything to do with how he felt about her.

To keep this possibility from spoiling her good mood, she thought about last night. She could imagine what Bianca would say if she knew. *"You mean he was there all night and you still haven't kissed?"*

It wasn't as if they didn't want to. The look in his eyes told her he did. She knew he must have seen the same look in hers. It would happen when the time was right, she thought.

And then what?

She felt as if she were being pulled in two opposite directions. Did she want this relationship with Nick to progress, or didn't she?

Nita arrived. "I didn't expect you'd be here this morning," she said, giving Tracey a hug. "We heard Grymes Hill had a rough time. Was it scary? I wanted to call you but we don't have a cell phone. How did you get off the hill? We heard the roads were blocked by fallen trees."

"I walked part way and got a lift to the ferry," Tracey replied.

She didn't want to tell Nita yet about Nick coming to them in the storm last night. Nita would only squeal with delight and start chattering about a romance. She felt mixed-up enough without that.

But there was nothing mixed-up about her next thought. It flashed into her mind with the utmost clarity. How could she wait until Saturday to see Nick again?

Chapter Seven

At the studios, only a few co-workers seemed aware of the severity of last night's storm, and even those few had no idea it had devastated the area where she lived. She was greeted with remarks such as, "Hey, you had a little rain out on Staten Island, didn't you?"

She didn't tell anyone how bad it had been, and went to the meeting scheduled for ten o'clock, just as if this morning were no different than any other. But it was unlike any other morning she'd ever known. Her walk with Nick over the rubble-strewn streets to his truck would stay in her memory always.

"Road of Life" 's producer presided at the meeting. He announced that viewer response to Bianca Morelli's role as the seductive Emerald Drake had been extremely positive and ratings were up since her first appearance on the show. "She's become the woman they love to hate," he said, "so we're beefing up the part. As soon as our writers can do it, the naughty Emerald will be seen more often."

How excited Bianca would be when they told her, Tracey thought. She recalled Nick saying his mother and aunt watched soap operas and he was going to tell them he knew someone who knew the sultry siren on "Road of Life." No matter how a thought started out in her mind, it always led to Nick.

During the afternoon, Larry phoned. She thought he sounded somewhat annoyed. "I'm glad you weathered the storm," he said. "I would have given you a call last night, but by the time I found out how bad it was on Grymes Hill, I thought you'd probably be asleep.

"Well, thanks for the thought," she replied. "How did you know I'd made it to work?"

"I called your home number a few minutes ago and got your mother."

"So, the phones are back on. That's good," she said.

"Yes. Your mother said yours was back in service around noon. I was surprised when she told me you'd gone to work. I heard the hill roads were blocked by fallen trees."

What else had Mother told him? She imagined Larry listening to a full account of last night's happenings. Knowing Mother was not fond of Larry, she wouldn't put it past her to let him know Nick was not only thoughtful and brave, but also young and handsome.

"A friend helped me get off the hill and gave me a lift to the ferry." she said.

"That's what your mother told me," he replied. The tone of his voice indicated Mother had not held back a single detail.

"I got the impression both you and your mother think this fellow is some kind of hero," he added. Tracey noticed *hero* rolled off his tongue dripping with sarcasm.

"He cared enough about us to come out in the storm to see if we were okay." she said.

"I see," he replied. "And I suppose you're sore at me because I didn't phone you. I'm surprised at you, Tracey. You've always been able to take care of yourself."

She wanted to tell him to wise up and realize no matter how independent a modern woman might be, she could appreciate some good, old-fashioned chivalry. Instead, she said, "I'm not sore at you, but I can't talk anymore right now. I'm up to my neck in work."

"All right," he said, "but before I hang up, how about going to the golf dinner and dance at the country club Saturday night?"

"Sorry, I can't make it. But thanks anyway," she replied.

After a silence during which she could almost feel icicles forming on the line, he replied. "I get it. Okay, if that's the way you want it. Goodbye, Tracey."

She hung up the phone knowing she'd burned her

bridges as far as Larry was concerned. Again, she felt besieged by mixed feelings. Part of her told her she shouldn't have brushed off a man who fit so perfectly into her life. Another part responded by saying her life was different now. Nick had turned it upside-down and it would never be the same again. Still another part reminded her of Nick's attachment to his mother, and warned it could cause trouble if she allowed their relationship to progress.

By the time she headed for home, she felt more confused than ever.

Mother picked her up at the ferry in the Blue Bomb.

"Things are pretty much back to normal," she said. "The insurance company's sending someone around tomorrow to see about the damage." She laughed. "Would you believe some of our poolside furniture was blown clear over to the Hamiltons' yard? They brought it back this afternoon. They said they lost a tree and some shutters were ripped off their house. And part of the Millers' roof was blown off, and. . . ."

Tracey waited until the full report of neighborhood damage had been completed before saying Larry had phoned her at work. "Oh," Mother said, as she turned the Blue Bomb from Bay Street onto Victory Boulevard. "I guess he told you he phoned the house first."

"Yes, he did. I gathered you told him about Nick coming out in the storm to check on us and staying all night."

"Of course I told him. It irks me every time I think of him not calling you last night. I hope you don't mind my telling him about Nick."

"No, it's all right, Mom, but I'm curious. Exactly what did you tell him about Nick?"

"I didn't mention his name or anything else about him. I just said he was a new friend of yours and we were both very grateful to him," Mother replied. A moment later she added, "I hope this didn't cause trouble between you and Larry."

"You can call it trouble if you like," Tracey replied. "We won't be seeing Larry anymore."

Mother couldn't hold back a smile. "Well, I can't say I'm sorry," she said. "You know I never warmed up to him. He's too much like your father, putting his business before anything else."

For a moment Tracey thought Mother was on the verge of one of her bitter tirades. Instead, she started talking about Nick.

"I've become very fond of him," she said. "I know there's something going on between you two, and I hope you're not going to use that mama's boy nonsense as an excuse to break it off."

With her conflicting thoughts still plaguing her, Tracey could not reply. But it didn't matter. Mother came out with a remark on an entirely different subject.

"I've been thinking you should have a pool party and cookout before the summer is over," she said.

Tracey stared at her in surprise. Parties of any kind had become a thing of the past since Dad left.

"The gardener said he'd have the grounds cleared of storm debris by next weekend," Mother continued. "You could invite your friends to come the following Sunday evening. Will Nita be back from her wedding trip by then?"

Still dazed, Tracey nodded. "Yes, they'll be back that Saturday."

"Good," Mother said. "Maybe you'd like it to be a party in honor of the newlyweds. How does it sound to you, dear?"

It sounded as if Mother had undergone a transformation, Tracey thought. "Good idea, Mom," she said, "but aren't you going to invite some of your friends, too?"

For a moment she wished she hadn't asked. "No," Mother said. "All my so-called friends have dropped me since your father abandoned us."

There was no use telling her she hadn't been dropped by her friends; she'd withdrawn from them herself, Tracey thought. She hoped the question hadn't stirred up a bitter tirade against Dad.

It hadn't. Mother resumed her talk about the party as if the question had not been asked. "I know all your friends will enjoy meeting Nick," she said, turning the wagon off Victory Boulevard onto the road leading up the hill.

Was this a scheme to establish Nick as the man in

her life? Tracey wondered. True or not, one thing was certain. Nick had drawn Mother farther out of her shell than she could ever have imagined.

While they watched television after dinner, the phone rang. Mother picked it up, saying "It's probably Nick calling to ask if everything's back to normal here."

It was Nick. "Yes, we're all hooked up again now," Mother said. "You were thoughtful to call. Tracey and I were just talking about having a pool party the Sunday after next. We hope you can come. You can? Wonderful. I know you want to talk to Tracey, so I'll put her on." She handed the phone to Tracey and said she had something to attend to in the kitchen.

"Hello, Tracey," he said. "So, you're having a pool party. Does that mean your mother's decided to get back with her old friends?"

"Unfortunately, no. The party will include my friends only," Tracey replied. She glanced around to make sure Mother was still out of the room. "When I suggested asking hers, she wouldn't hear of it. But I'm delighted anyway. I'd given up hoping there'd ever be a party in this house again. It's your influence. She started coming out of her shell the first time she met you."

"Your mother is a likeable lady," he said. "And so's her daughter. Have you recovered from our hike this morning?"

Hearing him ask about their walk sent her heart into its now-familiar spin. She could almost feel the gentle pressure of his hand with hers.

"Fully recovered," she replied. But that wasn't true. She'd never get over the feelings their walk had stirred in her heart. "Thanks so much for getting me to the ferry, Nick," she added. "If it hadn't been for you I would have missed a meeting."

Suddenly she thought of the announcement about Bianca. "Remember my telling you about a friend who plays a sultry siren on 'Road of Life'?" she asked.

"The actress with the Italian name? Sure I remember," he replied. "I mentioned her to my mother and aunt and they knew exactly who I was talking about. Aunt Tessie said she's a vamp. Mother used a less conservative word. What's up with your friend?"

"She's done such a good job of it, the part's going to be expanded. Your mother and aunt will see a lot more of Emerald Drake from now on."

"Emerald Drake," he said with a laugh. "How do they come up with those names? I'll be sure and tell Mother and Aunt Tessie."

"Was your mother worried about you last night?" she asked.

"You know how mothers are. They always worry," he replied. "But I didn't call you to talk about your actress friend or my mother. I wanted to tell you it's too long till Saturday night. I don't want to wait till then to see you again."

All she could manage to say was "Okay."

"How about tomorrow night?" he asked.

"Okay," she said again.

"I'm working late, so it can't be a dinner date. I won't get there till about eight-thirty."

"Fine. I'm having lunch with my father tomorrow and that's all the fancy feeding I can handle in one day. We don't have to go out. We can talk and watch TV."

"Have you decided to take my advice and ask your father why he wanted a divorce?"

"Maybe I'll ask him tomorrow."

"I know this has been troubling you," he said. "Whatever the reason, you'd feel better knowing."

"I'll think about it," she replied.

After they said goodnight, she sat by the phone for several minutes, trying to sort out her thoughts and emotions. Wanting to see her before Saturday night and wanting her to be free of her puzzlement about the divorce were two more ways Nick had shown he cared about her. Caring. That was the foundation of a good relationship, and Nick had an abundance of it in him.

She'd never come so close to telling herself his attachment to his mother didn't matter.

Chapter Eight

Dad regarded her across his regular table in the posh downtown restaurant. "You look even prettier than usual today, sweetheart," he said.

He'd picked up on her mood, Tracey thought. Her heart had been soaring ever since last night. Every time she thought of seeing Nick tonight, it flew a little higher. "Thanks, Dad," she replied.

Dad perused the menu. "I'm going to order the beef Wellington," he said. "What looks good to you, sweetheart?"

She scanned her own menu. "Last time I was here I had the lobster salad. I think I'll order it again. It was delicious."

"And fruit compote for both of us to start with, as usual?" he asked.

Fruit compote at Dad's favorite restaurant was not a collection straight out of can. It included fresh strawberries, pineapple, peaches and grapes. They ordered it every time they lunched here.

"Fruit compote, of course," she replied, with a big smile.

Dad gave the hovering waiter their order and settled back in his chair. "I heard Staten Island was hit with a bad storm while I was in London," he said. "Is everything okay at the house?"

She told him about the tree smashing through the den window. "That was the only damage. We were lucky. Some of the neighbors had much worse."

"You and your mother must have been terrified."

"Yes, we were both scared, but. . . ." She told him about Nick coming to check on them. Putting her recollections of that night into words strengthened the feelings about Nick she'd had then and since. He cared about her. Shouldn't that be all that mattered?

"This Nick must be a fine young man," Dad said. "Tell me some more about him."

Their first course was served at that moment, but the interruption did not divert Dad. "I want to hear more about this young man, Tracey," he said.

"Well, I met him when I was driving Mom's Buick wagon and it broke down on Victory Boulevard," she began.

He frowned. "She still has the Blue Streak?"

"Yes," Tracey replied. She didn't mention that she and Mother had renamed it the Blue Bomb.

"Why weren't you driving your Mercedes?" he asked.

"Mom had to pick up some people at the ferry who'd come to look at a big house so I loaned her the Mercedes. It was lucky I did. If she'd picked them up in the wagon and it broke down, it would have been very embarrassing."

Dad speared a strawberry and shook his head. "There's no excuse for your mother having an unreliable car. And I don't like the idea of you driving it while she borrows your Mercedes."

"It doesn't happen often, Dad."

He smiled. "I shouldn't begrudge your mother the use of a good car now and then, though I don't know why she hasn't gotten one for herself."

Dad mustn't suspect, as she did, that Mother hung onto the Blue Bomb because it represented happier days, Tracey thought. "Mom likes the wagon and it still runs okay," she said.

He frowned. "Didn't you tell me it broke down while you were driving it?"

"Well, yes, it did, but. . . ."

"We got off the subject back there," he said. "You were telling me that's how you met this young man."

He listened while Tracey recounted her first meeting with Nick. The fruit compote was eaten and replaced with her lobster salad while she talked. By the time they'd finished their main course, she'd started to describe Nick's female-friendly shop. By the time dessert was served, an expression of approval appeared on Dad's face.

"I'd say this Nick is an enterprising young fellow," he said, looking at her over his cherry cheesecake. "I like everything else you told me about him, too. Tell me, sweetheart, is he the reason for the sparkle in your eyes?"

The question caught her in the middle of a spoonful of crème brûlée. She had a moment to consider an answer. If she told him she was only a step away from the "L" word, he'd want to know what was holding her back.

"I like him more than any man I've ever known," she said. "And Mom's crazy about him."

Dad laughed, as if he thought she'd transposed her own feelings with Mother's. "I'd like to meet him," he said. "I'll be out of the country off and on for the next two weeks, but we'll set something up after that."

"Okay, Dad," she said. She wanted Dad and Nick to meet. Dad had already guessed Nick wasn't just a casual acquaintance. Nick's phone call last night had mellowed her misgivings about his attachment to his mother. Knowing he cared about her should be all that mattered, she thought. And in two weeks she might be ready to admit to herself and to Dad how she really felt about him.

Suddenly, she remembered Nick's question on the phone last night. Was she going to ask Dad why he ended the marriage? She knew Nick had urged her to ask him because he wanted her to be free of the puzzlement she'd lived with for nine years.

Dad had only started eating his dessert and had barely touched his coffee. She couldn't tell herself there wasn't enough time. She took a deep breath. "Dad," she said, "there's something I've wondered about for nine years. You said you'd tell me, but you must have forgotten. . . ."

The look in his eyes told her he knew what she meant. "I didn't forget, sweetheart," he said. "I intended to tell you, but I kept putting it off. Time passed, and when you didn't ask me about it again, I thought it didn't matter to you anymore."

"I never stopped wondering what happened. Sometimes I thought it was something I'd done," she said.

She could see his own pain in his eyes as he shook his head. "My dear little girl, what pain I put you through. You had nothing to do with it. It was strictly a matter between your mother and me. It's a long story but what it boils down to is that I couldn't live with her anymore."

She thought of Mother—pretty, funny, intelligent and as much in the dark as she. "Mom doesn't know why you couldn't live with her anymore," she said.

He looked startled. "She *should* know. She talked about it often enough. Let me tell you the whole story, Tracey. First, I want you to know I loved your mother very much. When we first met I thought she was the prettiest and smartest. . . ." He gave a deep sigh. "She was fresh out of college when we met. Both of us came to Manhattan from the Midwest and worked for the same investment firm as stockbrokers. Neither of us made much money, but we got married and managed on our combined incomes."

He gave Tracey a reassuring smile. "I know you're anxious for me to answer your question, sweetheart, but before I do I have to fill you in on the background."

"I never knew Mom was once a stockbroker," Tracey said. "She never talks about it. I wonder why she didn't go back to doing that instead of going into real estate."

Dad chuckled. "She's doing much better in real estate than she did as a stockbroker. Though she was smart as a whip with a degree in business, she just wasn't any good at it."

Tracey thought of Dad's financial accomplishments, the firm he'd founded, the international conglomerate he'd developed and the Manhattan tower which bore his name. She thought of his material wealth, his Park Avenue penthouse, his chauffeured limousine, his fully-crewed yacht. . . .

"But you were very good at it, weren't you, Dad?" It was more of a statement than a question.

"Yes, I was good at it, even though I never went to college," he said. "The firm took me on and trained me during a bull market when they needed brokers. A year after your mother and I were married, my commissions doubled hers. She used to laugh about it—she, the college graduate making less than her high school graduate husband. Then one of the firm's executives noticed my record. He became my mentor, and in another two years I was able to buy the Grymes Hill house."

"That's the year I was born, wasn't it?" Tracey asked.

"Right. That was a great year. Your mother stopped working and stayed home to take care of you. She said she wasn't getting anywhere with her job and we didn't need her income anymore. She used to make jokes about the value of a college degree versus a high school diploma."

Mother's jokes might have come from resentment, Tracey thought.

"We settled into a nice life on Staten Island," Dad continued. "I joined the Richmond County Country Club. Your mother and I both played golf. We acquired a host of friends. We weren't wealthy, but we were financially well-off. It was around that time I noticed your Mother's jokes about her college degree became more like jabs at me for not having the same level of education as she. The remarks escalated, but even though they hurt, I tried to laugh them off. You were growing into a delightful little girl, Tracey, and I concentrated on having a good family life."

"We had some wonderful times," Tracey replied. "I'll never forget the camping trips."

Dad smiled. "Yes, those were happy years, but they would have been a whole lot happier if your mother hadn't persisted in bringing up my lack of education every chance she got."

Why would Mother denigrate Dad like that? Tracey wondered. *She should have admired and respected him for being able to provide her with a beautiful home and all the trimmings, despite the fact he'd never gone beyond high school.*

Dad must have sensed the question in her mind. "I asked myself, again and again, why your mother kept making those remarks. Finally I decided I'd show her what I could do on my high school education. I was determined to make a lot of money. I thought she'd quit needling me then."

"That's when you started working late and on weekends, and going away on business trips," Tracey said. "I remember the first summer you didn't have time to take us camping."

"I missed our family life, sweetheart, but I had my mind set on making so much money that your mother wouldn't ridicule me anymore. Well, I made money, all right, more than I ever dreamed of having. I didn't stop after my first million. I wheeled and dealed until I was worth close to a billion."

He gave a wan smile. "Do you know what your mother said when I told her I'd just closed my first multi-million dollar deal? She called me a twelfth-grade tycoon."

"I remember that," Tracey said. "I didn't know what it meant."

"What it meant was your mother considered herself superior to me because she had a college degree and I had a high school diploma," he replied. "I knew then that she'd never let up on the needling. That was the beginning of the end of our marriage. I stuck around for awhile longer, but the time finally came when I knew I couldn't take it anymore."

He reached across the table and pressed her hand. "I still loved your mother when I left, sweetheart. I remember thinking, as I went out the door, if she'd only say she'd never fling her college degree in my face again, I'd turn around and take her in my arms."

Tracey felt the sting of tears. "Oh, Dad. How could Mom not know what she was doing to you? How could she not know that's why you left?"

He shook his head. "I thought she knew. I told her more than once how I felt."

"She thinks your frequent absences from home caused the breakup."

"There wouldn't have been frequent absences from home if I wasn't bent on proving I could make a lot of money without any college." He paused, looking into her eyes. "Are you going to tell her?"

"Should I, after all this time?"

"If she really doesn't know why I left, it might bring closure."

"I'll think long and hard about it," Tracey said.

She thought about it in the limo, after kissing Dad goodbye. She pondered on it during the rest of the day, and on her way home on the subway and ferry. Under Nick's influence, Mother had started to come out of her shell. Would this drive her back in?

Dad's explanation had put an end to a thought she'd held for nine years. He hadn't simply stopped loving Mother. Knowing this made her feel more trusting of men. But how would it make Mother feel?

She'd talk it over with Nick tonight, she decided. The thought of seeing him made her heart sing.

"What time is Nick coming over?" Mother asked at dinner.

"Around eight-thirty. He's working late," Tracey replied. She hadn't even mentioned she'd had lunch with Dad. She didn't want to risk sending Mother into one of her bitter tirades or finding herself revealing what Dad had said. She wasn't ready to do that yet. She wanted to talk to Nick about it first.

How wonderful it was to know she could talk to him about something like this. It made his attachment to his mother seem unimportant. Mother was probably right; he was just being a good son.

Though she knew she'd see him in an hour, she felt as if she couldn't wait another minute.

The phone rang at quarter past eight. She picked it up. The instant she heard Nick's voice she knew something was wrong.

"Tracey, I hate doing this, but I can't see you tonight," he said.

Her disappointment was so great, she almost wept. Before she could ask him why, he told her.

"My mother had some kind of spell. I came home from the shop to change clothes and just as I was about to leave for your house, she keeled over and passed out for a couple of minutes. I called the doctor and he said bring her to the hospital emergency room. He's going to meet us there."

Disappointed as she was, Tracey felt genuine concern. "I'm sorry, Nick. I hope she'll be all right."

"Thanks, Tracey. She says she feels okay now, but I want the doctor to check her over. I'll call you tomorrow."

They said goodbye. She hung up the phone.

"I take it Nick's not coming. What's wrong?" Mother asked.

"His mother had a fainting spell and he's taking her to the emergency room."

"Oh, my. Did he have any idea what caused it?"

"No. He said she seems okay now, but he wants the doctor to examine her."

Mother nodded. "He's a good son."

Tracey hated herself for the thoughts that crept into her mind. Nick's mother might have faked the fainting spell to keep him from going to see the girl on Grymes Hill.

The mama's boy concept was back, stronger than ever.

Chapter Nine

"What's on your mind, dear? You're very quiet this morning," Mother said in the kitchen the next day,

"I didn't sleep well last night," Tracey replied.

Mother sighed as she handed Tracey a mug of coffee. "You were upset because Nick had to take his mother to the hospital, weren't you?"

"I was disappointed."

"It's more than that, I can tell," Mother said, seating herself at the kitchen table. "You think this is one more sign he's a mama's boy. That's foolish, Tracey. Any good son would have done the same thing."

Last night's thoughts still crowded Tracey's mind. She hated herself for thinking them, but they would not go away. Nick's mother could have faked her fainting spell to keep him from going out. Maybe he'd told her he was going to see his friends on Grymes Hill again and she'd put two and two together. If she was as possessive as Bianca's mother, she'd do anything to keep her boy tied to her apron strings.

"You're right, Mother, he did what he should have done," she said. *This would placate Mother,* she thought, *and keep her from suspecting what was bothering me.* She felt ashamed enough without Mother knowing.

She and Nita met on the 8:10 as usual. Ordinarily, Nita would pick up on her mood and demand to know what was troubling her. Today, she was too full of wedding chatter to notice anything.

"Did you ask Nick to escort you to the wedding?" she asked.

Tracey did not know how to reply. If Nick had kept their date last night, she would have asked him. She wasn't sure now if she'd ask him at all.

"Not yet," she said. To tell Nita she was leaning toward attending the wedding alone would be to stir up objections she didn't want to hear.

To divert Nita from the subject, she told her about the pool party, adding that Mother had suggested it be held in honor of the bride and groom.

Nita squealed with delight. "Oh, that's marvelous! It will be our first party as man and wife." She paused, and a quizzical look came over her face. "Are you sure your mother wants you to have a bunch of people over?"

Nita had known about Mother's social withdrawal since she and Tracey were fourteen. Tracey's birthday

fell on Halloween. That year Mother didn't give Tracey the usual Halloween birthday party with lighted
pumpkins all over the house and kids dressed in
spooky costumes. Tracey still remembered the feeling
of loss.

"It was all Mother's idea," Tracey said. "She's
come out of her shell far enough to want me to have
a pool party and a cookout."

"She wants you to start having your friends over
again. I'm glad, Tracey. You must be happy about
that."

Tracey nodded. "I'm very thankful."

Thankful to Nick.

No matter what happened, she'd always be grateful
to him. The thought saddened her. It was as though,
in her subconscious mind, she'd already decided his
attachment to his mother would make it impossible for
their relationship to develop.

Somehow she got through the day.

She and Mother had just finished dinner when the
phone rang. "That's probably Nick," she said. "I'll
take it in the den."

She answered. The sound of his voice sent her heart
into its usual spin.

"How's your mother?" she asked.

"She's fine. The doctor couldn't find anything that
might have caused her to pass out like that. He said
she needed to get more rest. I brought her home after

the doctor saw her. She didn't have to stay overnight in the hospital."

"I'm glad she's okay," Tracey said. It was difficult to say that when she still thought it might have been a fake fainting spell.

"I want to see you," he said. "How about tonight?"

"Don't you want to stay home and make sure your mother doesn't pass out again?" she asked. The instant she said it, she wished she hadn't. The words were weighted with obvious sarcasm.

She felt relieved when Nick didn't pick up on it. "She's okay, really, Tracey," he said. "She was in the kitchen early this morning making breakfast for the family just as though nothing had happend."

Probably because nothing had happened, Tracey thought. Again, she reproached herself for the thought.

"So how about it?" he asked. "May I come up for a little while? I need to see you."

She wanted to say she needed to see him, too. Instead, she told herself she needed to be alone, to think. "I had a very busy day at the studio and I'm really exhausted," she said.

He didn't answer right away. "Is something wrong, Tracey?" he asked.

To tell him there was nothing wrong would be lying. "I wouldn't be very good company tonight, Nick," she said.

"How about tomorrow night then?" he asked.

She forced a laugh. "We have a date for Saturday night, remember? We might as well wait till then."

She knew he'd be confused and hurt, but no more than she. It took every ounce of her will power not to tell him to forget what she'd said and get there as soon as he could.

"I thought *you* didn't want to wait till Saturday either," he said.

"Well, I do now," she replied. She knew she sounded curt, but she had to end the conversation before she gave in.

She could hear the puzzlement in his voice. "All right. I'll see you Saturday."

She hung up the phone and brushed at her eyes just as Mother came into the room. "Is Nick coming over tonight?" she asked.

"No, not tonight," Tracey replied, hoping Mother wouldn't notice the tears.

"You look as if you've been crying," Mother said. "Oh, don't tell me it's about Nick's mother. What happened at the hospital last night?"

"His mother's fine," Tracey replied. "The doctor couldn't find a thing wrong with her."

"That's good." Mother cast her a penetrating look. "I'm surprised you're so emotional about it."

Let Mother think she'd shed tears of relief. She didn't want to talk about Nick and his mother. She only wanted to go to her room to relax and think.

"Mom, I'm going to take a hot bath and turn in early," she said.

"That's a good idea, dear," Mother replied. "You look tired. I think I'll watch TV down here awhile before I go upstairs."

The hot bath didn't relax Tracey as much as she'd hoped. It was her mind that needed relaxing, she decided. Instead of letting her mind churn with thoughts of Nick and his mother, she should read something light.

In pajamas and a robe, she curled up on her chaise lounge with the new issue of *Town and Country*. Maybe reading about the latest fashions and the most sought after vacation spots would take her mind off that regrettable phone conversation with Nick.

It didn't. She couldn't concentrate. The hurtful words she'd said to him still echoed in her mind. If only she could take them back. Her need to see him was so acute it was almost painful.

She threw down the magazine and went to her window. The night was cool and clear. Below, the pool shimmered in the light of a half moon.

Maybe if she went down and walked around the pool she'd feel better, she thought. She knew she couldn't feel any worse.

Mother was still in the den watching television. "I'm going out to the pool for awhile, Mom," she said.

"I hope you're not thinking of going for a swim,

dear," Mother said. "The water's still full of twigs and leaves."

"No, Mom, I'm just going to walk around."

"In your pajamas and robe?"

"Why not? Nobody's going to see me. Anyway, I'm more modest in my pj's and robe than in my bikini."

"That's the truth," Mother said, with a laugh.

Outside, she strolled the length of the pool, feeling the touch of a cool breeze upon her face. She paused to look up at the sky, star-studded around the half moon. *What a beautiful night,* she thought. *It was hard to believe that only two nights ago a savage storm had raged here. It was as though Mother Nature, ashamed of her tantrum, was now trying to make amends.*

Her longing to see Nick intensified. At that moment nothing else mattered.

She heard Mother calling her name, but when she turned around it wasn't Mother she saw, but Nick. He strode toward her. With her heart racing, she almost ran to meet him.

"Are you going to tell me you just happened to be in the neighborhood?" she asked.

"No," he replied. "I'm going to tell you I had to see you. Before you throw me out, I want to know what's wrong."

The moonlight glanced in his eyes and she could see that caring look. She caught the scent of his aftershave. She sensed the magnetism that had drawn her to him from their first meeting.

He didn't wait for her to answer, but brought her to him and enfolded her in his arms, so closely that she could not tell if the joyful heartbeats were her own or his. He looked into her eyes for an instant before they kissed.

She'd never imagined a kiss could be like this. In it, she felt the depth of his caring.

He held her close for a moment before he spoke. "Whatever was wrong, is it all right now?"

"Yes," she said. It *was* all right. She would not spoil this joyous moment by thinking beyond now.

They sat down on a bench. He took her hands in his. "I'm not going to ask you any questions, Tracey. You can tell me sometime, when whatever it was doesn't matter anymore."

His empathy touched her heart. *He is as under-standing as Dad,* she thought.

As though he knew she'd thought of her father, Nick said, "You said you were having lunch with your dad today. How did it go?"

She knew he meant had she asked him about the reason for the divorce.

"I asked him and he told me," she said. "You were so right. I feel a whole lot better knowing."

"Are you going to tell your mother?" he asked.

"Dad asked me the same question. He thinks I should."

Nick must be curious, she thought, *but he made no attempt to find out why Dad wanted to end the marriage.* He was a no-pressure kind of man. This was another of his traits she liked.

"I want you to know, too," she said. She told him the whole sad story, leaving nothing out, looking into his eyes as she spoke the final words. "He still loved my mother when he left. He just couldn't live with the needling any more."

Nick shook his head. "That divorce never should have happened. If your father had been more forceful—if he'd made her understand what her remarks were doing to him, they could have worked it out. Instead, he thought the solution would be to show her what a man could achieve without a college degree."

"And that only eroded the marriage further," Tracey added.

He looked at her with a playful grin. "Lucky for me I'm a college graduate."

She laughed. He always seemed to know when to inject a little humor into a serious talk. But might there be a hidden meaning in the remark? Had the thought of marriage crossed his mind, as it had hers? She thrust the idea away. She hadn't fully accepted the "L" word yet. Even their kiss hadn't swept away the obstacle of his mother's hold on him.

His hand traced the embroidered flowers on her robe. "You said you were tired and I can see you're ready to turn in. I guess I'd better go home."

She wanted him to stay but didn't urge him. She sensed a few more minutes would mean a few more kisses, and things had moved fast enough tonight.

They walked through the house to the front door. He put his arms around her and looked into her eyes.

"Can we hold out till Saturday night?"

She laughed. "I can if you can."

"I'll call you tomorrow night," he said. His arms tightened around her. His mouth sought hers and she felt her heart come together with his in the kiss.

Chapter Ten

Tracey awoke the next morning feeling more mixed-up than ever. But it was a happy confusion. She found herself humming the melody of an old Beetles love song as she dressed.

On the ferry, Nita curtailed her pre-wedding prattle long enough to say, "You look wonderful today, Tracey. Are you wearing a new kind of makeup?"

"No, I'm just feeling great," she replied. *There is no makeup to equal a happy heart,* she thought.

Before Nita got going on her bride talk, Tracey told her she'd decided to ask Nick to escort her to the wedding. "I'm asking him tomorrow night," she said.

"I knew you would," Nita said with a delighted squeal. Fortunately, her approaching wedding occupied too much of her mind for her to dwell on this. She didn't even mention a possible romance, but got right back to nuptial prattle.

At work, the morning was busy. Tracey didn't have time for wandering thoughts. It wasn't until afternoon that she was able let her mind review last night again.

She'd never felt so happy. Only one thing kept her from absolute bliss. Like a tiny flaw in a beautifully-woven tapestry, the thought of Nick's mother marred the perfection.

She could not get it out of her mind that the fainting spell may have been faked.

At that moment, Bianca came into the office. Tracey hadn't seen her since her role on "Road of Life" had been expanded.

"Hello, Emerald, I hear you're going to be stealing more husbands than ever on the show," she said.

"Isn't it fantastic? I'm still pinching myself to make sure I'm not having a glorious dream," Bianca replied. Her dark eyes scrutinized Tracey. "You look as though something glorious has happened to you, too. Let me guess. You and the Italian Stallion have made some progress."

"You guessed right," Tracey said.

Bianca pulled a chair near Tracey's desk and sat down. "So, did you finally get around to kissing him?"

Tracey felt a sudden warmth in her face. She wished she didn't have this tendency to blush. It was a dead giveaway.

"You *did*," Bianca said. "And . . . ?"

"And I've decided to ask him to that wedding," Tracey replied. She knew it wasn't the answer Bianca wanted to hear, but she didn't want to reveal the secrets of her heart.

"How are you getting along with his mother?" Bianca asked.

"I haven't met his mother yet," Tracey replied.

Something in her voice must have alerted Bianca. "But there's a problem anyway, right?" she asked. "What's she been doing to keep him from seeing you?"

Bianca was an expert when it came to possessive mothers. It was as if she knew exactly what had happened. "Did your mother ever do things to keep your brother from seeing his girlfriend?" she asked.

Bianca laughed. "All the time. What's this one done?"

"I'm not certain she did anything," Tracey replied. "But the other night, just as Nick was about to leave his house to keep a date with me, she had a fainting spell and Nick had to take her to the hospital."

Bianca nodded her head. "But the doctor couldn't find anything wrong with her, could he?"

"No. Nick told me she was up early the next morning, making breakfast for the family."

"And putting away a stack of pancakes with sausage and three eggs over easy, I'll bet," Bianca said.

"You mean, your mother . . . ?"

"Sure, she pulled that stunt on Michael more than once. He never did wise up."

Tracey couldn't imagine Nick not wising up. The

trick might work once, but he was too smart to be fooled again.

Bianca seemed to know what she was thinking. "Don't imagine for one minute that your Nick's any smarter than my brother where their mamas are concerned," she said.

Tracey sighed. "How am I going to handle this, Bianca?"

"Well, Sandra handled it by getting Michael to elope. She wanted to have her own minister and our priest perform an ecumenical ceremony in the Catholic church, but I guess she knew Mother would think of some way to stop it—like faking a seizure in the church."

"Is that the only reason your mother doesn't like Sandra—because she's not Catholic?"

"Well, it didn't help that she's only half-Italian," Bianca replied. She looked at Tracey with a wry smile. "You've got more strikes against you than she does."

She rose from her chair. "Well, I know you've got work to do, so I'll run along. Have a good weekend, Tracey." With a wave of a magenta-nailed hand, she was out the door, leaving Tracey to mull over everything she'd said.

She told herself she should not worry about religious and ethnic differences. Marriage was the remotest of possibilities. The thought of it had flashed into her mind, as unwelcome as a streak of lightning.

On her way home on the subway and ferry, she

pondered further. The idea of commitment had never complicated her feelings before. Why should it concern her now? Without marriage, there'd be no problem of her being or not being Catholic or Italian. Why couldn't she and Nick go on as they were?

She knew the answer before she asked the question. She knew they could not go on as they were. Their relationship had already gone beyond any she'd ever known, and she knew in her heart Nick was not the kind of man who'd allow it to go further without a lifetime commitment.

Serious as these thoughts were, they could not dim the shining happiness within her. Her mood was still bright with the memory of last night.

But she felt thankful they'd agreed not to see one another until tomorrow night. She needed time to think.

Apparently Mother sensed that things had progressed with Nick. She made no attempt to hide the fact that she was pleased.

"I almost feel as if Nick's my son," she said as she and Tracey ate breakfast Saturday morning.

A strong wish passed through Tracey's mind. If only Nick's mother could feel that way about her. How much had Nick said about her to his mother? *Enough to have her fake a fainting spell,* she thought.

But like yesterday, these thoughts could not tarnish

her happiness. She found heself counting the hours till she would see him again.

"Where are you going for dinner tonight?" Mother asked as Tracey came into the den dressed to go out.

"I don't know," Tracey replied. Nor did she care. All she wanted was to sit across a table from him and look into his eyes and see his smile and hear his voice and feel the touch of his hand.

Mother glanced toward the window. "There's a car coming into the drive. It's not Nick's truck."

Tracey remembered he'd told her he'd borrow his mother's car for tonight. "The car belongs to his mother," she said. "He thought I wouldn't like to go out to dinner in a commercial truck, so he borrowed hers."

Did his mother know he was taking the Grymes Hill girl on a date in her car? she wondered.

"I hope you didn't give him the idea you'd be ashamed to be seen in a truck, dear," Mother said. "That would have been insufferably snobbish."

"Mom, you and Dad taught me to think better than that."

She saw Mother stiffen at the mention of Dad, but at that moment the doorbell sounded, fending off any caustic remarks.

Though she'd carried the imagery of Nick around in her mind ever since the night at poolside, the sight of him in person was overwhelming. She felt almost bashful.

Mother greeted him with a kiss. "Hello, Nick. Tracey told me your mother gave you a scare the other night. How is she?"

"She's fine, thanks, Mrs. Wood. The doctor couldn't find anything wrong. We think it might have been a combination of the heat and getting overtired. She'd cooked a big dinner and the kitchen was still hot while she was cleaning up."

"I'm glad it wasn't anything serious," Mother said.

It was evident Mother didn't suspect a fake fainting spell.

"It was nice of your mother to lend you her car," she said as Nick helped her into a late-model Honda.

"She seldom uses it, except to go and play cards with friends once in awhile," he replied.

She wanted to ask him if she knew her car was being used to take a girl out for dinner. Instead, she told herself to stop thinking about his mother.

"Where are we going?" she asked as he turned the Honda off the hill.

"There's a place over on the North Shore I think you'll enjoy. Maybe you've been there. It's right on the Kill Van Kull and you can see part of the Manhattan skyline and watch boats go by right outside the windows."

She knew the place. She'd been there twice with Larry, but she didn't tell him.

"I like the sound of it," she said.

He nodded. "It has a nice atmosphere and the food's excellent. I service the owner's cars. That's how I heard about it."

"Have you been there often?"

"Just once. The family took Mother there for her birthday a few weeks ago." He glanced at her. "Speaking of mothers, have you decided whether you're going to tell yours about your talk with your father?"

"No, I haven't. She's like a different person since she met you, Nick. I want her to stay this way. I'm afraid if I tell her, she'll be so shocked she'll crawl back in her shell again."

"Did she used to socialize a lot?"

"Oh, yes. She and Dad had a lot of friends. They played golf, partied, entertained at home. And Mother played bridge and was active in our church and did volunteer work at the hospital."

"And she just dropped out of everything?"

"That's right. This pool party she's planning will be a breakthrough. You've been a good influence on her."

He smiled. "I'm glad she likes me. I like her, too. She'd make a great mother-in-law."

How could she snuff out that marriage thought when he came out with such remarks? She laughed, pretending the thought had never occurred to her. "Mother would be pleased to hear you say that," she said.

In the restaurant, they were shown to a table next to a window. As Nick helped her be seated, she remembered the last time she'd been here. While she'd struggled to get her chair closer to the table, Larry turned his attention to a tugboat and barge sailing past.

"Shall we have wine with our dinner, or would you rather not?" Nick asked.

"I have no objections to wine now and then," she replied.

"Good," he said. "This is kind of a celebration for us. It was a week ago today that I saw a pretty blonde in distress on Victory Boulevard."

"It seems much longer than a week ago," she said. Hearing him say "pretty blonde in distress" made her remember how sure she'd been of his sexist tendencies. Now, she'd almost forgotten about it. She found herself wishing the time would come when she could forget about his attachment to his mother.

When their food and wine were served, he raised his glass. "Here's to one week ago today," he said.

They touched glasses and settled down to their meal.

"How's the friend you were on your way to see that day?" he asked. "You said she was getting married soon"

"She's a very happy bride-to-be. Her wedding is a week from today," Tracey replied. Suddenly she remembered her decision to ask him to escort her to the wedding. "Nita expects me to bring someone. Would you like to be my escort?" she asked.

He didn't hesitate for an instant. "Yes, I would," he

said. "I remember you saying it's going to be an afternoon wedding, so I won't have to play hookey from work."

"You'd play hookey to escort me to a wedding?"

"Sure I would. What time is the ceremony?"

"Four o'clock. The reception's right after that at the country club."

"Speaking of weddings, one of my sisters is getting married in a few weeks. How about returning me the favor?"

"You want to take me to your sister's wedding?"

"Yes. Will you go with me?"

"What will your . . . family think. They don't even know me."

"I guess it's time they met you. I'll arrange it. But you haven't answered my question. May I take you to Estelle's wedding?"

"Yes, you may," she replied. "Just give me the details so I'll know how to dress."

"It's the second Saturday in September at noon. The reception's at a catering hall following the ceremony."

"We're getting ourselves dated up pretty far ahead, aren't we?" she asked.

"Do you think we're moving too fast?"

"Well, not really, but you must admit we've come a long way in one week."

He reached across the table and took her hands. "Tracey," he said, looking into her eyes, "I don't play games."

In those few words, he'd described the essence of his character. He was a man who, when he saw what he wanted, did not hold back his effort to get it. He was honest and forthright in letting her know she was what he wanted. She knew if she put her trust in him she'd never regret it.

After dinner they drove around and talked. They never seemed to run out of things to talk about, she thought.

Back at the house, they went out to the pool and sat on the bench where they'd first kissed.

"We should call this the kissing bench," he said after they'd been there awhile. They laughed. Like their talking, they always seemed to have something to laugh about.

When at last they'd kissed goodnight, she watched the car until it disappeared into the darkness, and she asked herself how such a man could have been latched to his mother's apron strings. This question alone kept her from fully accepting what was in her heart.

Chapter Eleven

What a difference a week made, Tracey thought as she dressed for church the next morning.

Over the years, she'd drifted into a pleasant but unexciting weekly routine. Sundays were for church and visiting friends and tennis at the club in summer. Mondays through Fridays were centered on work, except for an occasional lunch or dinner with Dad and perhaps a movie date mid-week. Saturday afternoons she spent with Nita and other friends, and Saturday night was date night with whatever man happened to be in her life at the time. For the past several weeks it had been Larry.

It had seemed like a full life. Now, after one week of Nick, she knew if she had to go back to it, it would seem empty.

Today, Nick was picking her up after church and they'd drive down to the New Jersey shore. He wanted to show her an oceanfront area where he planned to buy a cottage someday. They'd have lunch in a seafood restaurant and browse through antique shops. An interest in antiques was among the many things they'd found they had in common.

On Monday night, Nick was coming up to the house for awhile. They'd watch television and talk and. . . . Remembering last night's kisses, she found herself wishing he were here with her this minute.

On Tuesday and Wednesday, he thought he'd have to work late. He was servicing cars for two of his best customers who'd planned cross-country vacations. If the hour wasn't too late when he finished, he'd drop by for a few minutes.

Mother had invited him for dinner on Thursday night and he'd suggested the three of them go to the outdoor concert in the park afterward. During their talks, they'd found out they both enjoyed classical music.

On Friday night, he wanted to show her his shop and then watch an old movie on television. Old movies were something else they'd discovered they both liked.

And Saturday was Nita's wedding.

Indeed, her life had changed since Nick had come into it. Smiling at the thought, she went downstairs to the kitchen. She and Mother had eaten breakfast earlier and she thought Mother would still be in her robe and slippers, reading the Sunday paper as usual. Mother had started skipping church soon after Dad left. Now she went only on Christmas and Easter. It was part of her withdrawal from the life she'd once led.

But this morning Tracey found her dressed for church and ready to go.

"I thought I'd go with you today, dear," she said. "But I don't want to stand around talking to people after the service. Promise me we'll go right to your car."

"Sure, Mom," Tracey replied. Though she could understand why Mom didn't want to talk to people immediately following the divorce, she should have gotten over it by this time. But her decision to go to church today was as much of a breakthrough as planning the pool party. It was another step out of her shell, she thought, and she knew it was partly due to Nick's influence.

Among the parishioners congregated outside the church after the service were a number of Mother and Dad's old friends. Tracey felt sure many of them were waiting for Mother to come out, hoping her presence here this morning meant she was ready to get back into her old life, hoping she'd stop and talk to them. But Mother acknowledged their greetings only with a wave and a smile as she walked straight to the Mercedes.

Still, it was a start, Tracey thought. *A week ago it wouldn't have happened. One week of Nick had made a difference in Mother's life, too.*

* * *

Saturday came. A morning of blue skies and sun-shine promised perfect weather for Nita's wedding, but it wouldn't have mattered to Tracey what the fore-cast might be. Rain or shine, all she could think of was going to the wedding with Nick.

He'd pick her up at three-thirty, he told her last night. That would give them plenty of time to get to the church. He'd borrow his mother's car again. "I couldn't let you be seen getting out of a repair truck in front of the country club," he said. "That would be even worse than trucking you to a restaurant."

He'd be more bothered about that than she, Tracey thought. Because she lived in a beautiful home in an affluent area, he thought she'd be ashamed of arriving at a country club reception in a commercial vehicle. Mother and Dad hadn't brought her up to think that way. She remembered Dad telling her a new car and a fancy house didn't necessarily mean you were any better off than someone who drove a jalopy and lived in a shack.

Nick still didn't know she drove a Mercedes. They hadn't gotten around to a serious discussion about cars yet. When he found out about the Mercedes, he'd be all the more reluctant to take her out in his truck.

She'd bought a new dress for the wedding—peri-winkle blue linen. And she'd wear the pearl necklace Dad had given her a few birthdays ago.

When she finished dressing, Mother came into her

bedroom. "You look lovely, dear," she said. "You and Nick will be a handsome couple."

It was nice having Mother call them a couple. She'd never referred to any of her other men friends like that, even the ones she seemed to like.

The sound of her cell phone came into her thoughts. She answered it, hoping it was Nick. She hadn't heard his voice today.

It was him. "Tracey, something's come up," he said. Her heart plummeted. Had his mother faked another spell? His next words put per fears to rest. "My mother needs her car this afternoon and one of my sisters is off somewhere with the other car. Could we use yours?"

"Sure. I'll pick you up in about half an hour."

"Thanks," he said. He gave her directions to his house, and then said, "Sorry for the short notice. My mother doesn't go out much and she forgot to tell me she needed the Honda today."

"No problem," Tracey said. *Forgot to tell him? A likely story,* she thought.

She'd take the Blue Bomb, she decided. This would show him she wasn't ashamed to be seen getting out of an aging wagon at the country club.

When she told Mother, Mother said she wanted to use the Blue Bomb to show some rural property. "The land will still be rough and muddy from the storm. I don't want to drive your car out there," she said.

Sooner or later, Nick would know about the Mer-

cedes, Tracey thought. She might as well get it over with.

On her way along Forest Avenue toward Nick's house, she wondered what his reaction would be when he found out Dad had given her a Mercedes as a graduation gift. Though cars were not uncommon on such occasions, they were generally in a lower price bracket. Nick would know right away that Dad was wealthy.

She had to laugh at herself. Being the daughter of a wealthy man was no disgrace. But she hoped he'd never find out about the international conglomerate.

When she turned into Nick's street, she saw him standing in front of a large frame house with a broad front porch. Her heart quickened at the sight of him. In a dark blue suit, white shirt and conservative tie, he looked as properly dressed for a country club reception as any junior member.

As she stopped the Mercedes, she saw him look it over from hood to trunk. She rolled down the window. "Hop in," she said.

"We've still got plenty of time," he said, eyes still taking in every detail of the Mercedes. "When I told Mother you were picking me up, she said bring you in to meet the family."

"Okay," she replied. *At last there was going to be a face attached to the phantom with the apron strings,* she thought.

As they went up the walk, he looked over his shoulder. "I didn't know you had a Mercedes," he said.

"My father gave it to me when I graduated from college," she replied.

At that moment the door to the house opened and a woman about Mother's age, small and slender with dark hair and eyes, came out onto the porch. Tracey had a moment's awareness of being appraised.

"So you're Dominick's friend from Grymes Hill," she said. As she spoke, Tracey saw her glance at the Mercedes.

Nick took Tracey's hand as they went up the porch steps. "Mother, this is Tracey Wood. Tracey, meet my mother," he said.

The woman smiled and extended her hand. "Gena Ferrone," she said as they shook hands. "Come in. Everyone wants to meet you. The only one not here is Estelle. She's off with the other car. That's why Nick couldn't come for you. I'm going out to play cards later."

Though she seemed pleasant, Tracey sensed a certain coolness. She followed Mrs. Ferrone into the house.

In the living room, six pairs of eyes scrutinized her. She was so overwhelmed that she only had a vague impression of the surroundings. She only saw that it was a comfortable-looking room with a large television screen.

"Meet Dominick's friend Tracey Wood from

Grymes Hill, everyone," his mother said. "Tracey, meet the family." She identified each by name. The two young women were Nick's sisters, Lucille and Frances. They bore a resemblance to Nick, and they seemed friendly.

Mrs. Ferrone placed her hand on the shoulder of a dark-haired woman, slightly older than she, who smiled and said, "Pleased to meet you.

"This is Dominick's Aunt Tessie," she said, before stepping over to an elderly couple seated on a sofa. "And here's his grandmother and grandfather."

The grandmother, a robust, gray-haired woman, nodded and smiled. The thin, graying grandfather didn't react at all, but just stared ahead at nothing in particular.

"Don't mind Grandpa, he's got Alzheimer's disease," Mrs. Ferrone whispered in her ear.

She turned and guided Tracey to a corner of the room. There, a man in a wheelchair looked up at her as Mrs. Ferrone introduced him. "This is my husband, Dominick's father, Paul Ferrone."

The man raised one of his hands and gave a twisted smile.

Again, Mrs. Ferrone whispered in her ear. "He had a stroke and he can't talk yet." She bent over and rearranged an afghan over his legs.

Tracey felt Nick's hand on her arm and heard his voice. "I guess I should have briefed you, but there wasn't time."

"Sit down, Tracey. Have coffee and pastries with us," Mrs. Ferrone said.

"Ma, we can't," Nick told her. "We're due at the church in ten minutes."

"Another time, then," his mother said.

"Thanks, Mrs. Ferrone, I'd like to come by again," Tracey said. She turned and waved at the assembled family members. "I'm glad to have met all of you."

Nick's mother accompanied them to the door and followed them out onto the porch. "I hope you have a good time at the wedding. Dominick said the bride's your best friend, Tracey."

"Yes, she is. We grew up together."

"I wish her good luck."

Her manner seemed cordial, but Tracey sensed an undercurrent of something other than genuine friendliness.

Nick gave his mother a kiss. "So long, Ma," he said.

"Goodbye, Mrs. Ferrone," Tracey said. She noticed Mrs. Ferrone was staring at the Mercedes.

On the way down the walk she handed the car keys to Nick. "Do you mind taking over the wheel? I don't like to drive with high heels."

"Driving that car will be tough, but I'll do it," he said with a grin.

In the car, he glanced at her with the trace of a frown. "Why didn't you tell me you had a Mercedes?"

"Why didn't you tell me your name's Dominick?" she replied.

He laughed. "There were a few other things I never got around to telling you."

"How long ago did your father have the stroke?" she asked.

"A couple of months ago. The doctors say he should recover to some extent. They say his speech will come back gradually."

"And your grandfather, how long has he had Alzheimer's?"

"It was diagnosed about a year and a half ago. It wasn't too bad at first, but it seems to be progressing."

She recalled he'd told her his mother should have more help running the house. Surely Mrs. Ferrone didn't take care of a stroke victim and an Alzheimer's patient in addition to the housekeeping. "Does a nurse come and help with your father and grandfather?" she asked.

He shook his head. "Mother insists on doing it herself. I hired a nurse when my father came home from the hospital, but Mother fired her the next day while I was at work. She said she doesn't want a stranger in her house and in her kitchen."

"She's carrying a heavy load, doing the cooking and cleaning and laundry for a big family and caring for two disabled men, too."

"That's not the half of it. Aunt Tessie's a diabetic and my grandmother has severe recurring arthritis, and Mother looks after them, too. And, as if that's not enough, now she's knocking herself out over my sister's wedding."

Tracey felt too stunned to speak. An enormous wave of guilt swept over her. Every mean thought she'd ever had about Nick's mother passed through her mind. No wonder she'd had a fainting spell the other night. The woman was exhausted.

Now she understood why Nick was so considerate of her. He wasn't a mama's boy tied to her apron strings. He was a good son. Mother had told her that more than once.

But the fact remained that there'd been no warmth in Mrs. Ferrone's manner. There'd been something lacking in her cordiality. Remembering her most recent talk with Bianca, she knew Nick's mother would never accept someone neither Italian nor Catholic. As Bianca had said, she had two strikes against her.

Now the problem of Nick's attachment to his mother had been replaced with his mother's dislike of her.

"You're very quiet," Nick said. "Was my family too much for you?"

"I was thinking about your mother," she replied. *That is no lie,* she thought.

The wedding reception began to wind down around nine o'clock.

Nita and Don had departed around seven-thirty, but

Nita's father had the band play as long as everyone was in a dancing mood.

"Wasn't it a lovely wedding, and didn't Nita look beautiful? Tracey asked Nick as they danced a slow waltz.

"Weddings are always lovely and brides always beautiful to loved ones," he replied.

"Why Dominick Ferrone, that was almost poetic!" she teased.

He laughed and tightened his arms around her. "You've brought out the poet in me. I could write a sonnet about you, Tracey Wood."

She tried to think of a flippant comeback, but his remark had touched her heart.

The band began to play an old tune, which signalled the end of the dancing was at hand.

"This was a first for us," Nick said.

"You're quite a dancer," she said.

"You're pretty light on your feet, yourself."

They'd had a wonderful time. She'd introduced Nick to her friends and they all seemed to get along. Nick ran into two men he'd known at Wagner. Tracey invited them all to the pool party. Altogether, the evening was a success. She didn't think about the new problem with Nick's mother until they walked to the car. She thrust it into a far corner of her mind. Like Scarlett O'Hara, she'd think about that tomorrow.

"I just remembered, you picked me up and you'll have to take me home," Nick said as they pulled away from the club. "I'm not ready to end the evening yet, are you?"

She wasn't sure she'd ever be ready to end it, she thought. For a few magical hours she'd been in a world apart from religious and ethnic differences.

"I don't want the evening to end either," she replied.

"When we get to my house I could jump in the truck and follow you home," he said. "It's another beautiful night. We could sit by the pool again."

The words were barely out of his mouth before she thought of the kissing bench.

Chapter Twelve

Tracey awoke the next morning with the same thought in her mind she'd had just before falling asleep last night. She'd come as close to the 'L' word as she should get.

She recalled something Nita had said. "Listen to yourself. You can't even *say* the word." She had to admit Nita was right. It was as if not saying the word would keep her from being caught up in its meaning.

The list of what Mother called excuses had dwindled, but the one added yesterday might as well be written in stone. Nick's mother did not like her. It would be folly to let things progress any further.

When she went downstairs to the kitchen, she found Mother already there. She'd started making breakfast and had just brought in the two Sunday newspapers, the *New York Times* and the *Staten Island Advance*.

As usual on Sundays, they ate breakfast before getting dressed for the day.

"Good morning, dear," Mother said. "Before we look at the papers, tell me all about the wedding,"

"Good morning, Mom. I would have told you about it last night, but your bedroom light was out. You must have turned in very early."

"I did," Mother said, pouring them each a mug of coffee. "I was tired after driving around for hours, showing woods and fields and old farmland."

"Are you going to church with me again?" Tracey asked.

Mother gave an emphatic shake of her head. "It bothered me, seeing everyone staring at me last Sunday. I know they were remembering how Dad walked out on me. It's not easy to hold your head up when everyone knows your husband stopped loving you. Now, tell me about the wedding."

Tracey did not try and reason with her. To do so would only bring on a bitter tirade. "The wedding was beautiful," she said. "Nita was a lovely bride, of course."

She remembered saying almost those same words to Nick. She couldn't go more than a few minutes without thinking of him.

"How was the reception? Did you have a good time?"

"We had a ball. There was a scrumptious buffet and

a great band that played everything—waltzes, swing, jazz, rock. Nick's a wonderful dancer."

"What are the two of you doing this afternoon?"

"A friend of his has a sailboat and he invited Nick to bring a date and go for a sail."

Mother smiled. "Never a dull moment since Nick came along," she said. "That man is one in a million. I hope you've stopped thinking he's a mama's boy."

"I know he's not. You were right, Mom. He's just a good son."

Mother's eyes shone with expectation. "Good sons make good husbands."

"Mom, you can put that idea out of your mind," Tracey said. "It's not that serious between Nick and me."

"You mean you don't want it to be that serious," Mother retorted. "What's holding you back, Tracey?"

"Please, let's just drop the subject, Mom," Tracey said. She knew Mom would call the newest problem with Nick's mother an excuse.

"It's because you don't trust men, isn't it?" Mother asked. "You think because your father abandoned me that Nick would do the same thing to you."

Tracey sensed the onset of a tirade against Dad. Now that she knew the truth about the divorce, she could not bear to listen. "It has nothing to do with Dad," she said. "I met Nick's family when I went to pick him up for the wedding. I found out his mother is a remarkable woman who takes care of a paralyzed husband and three other ailing family members besides doing all the housework. I can understand why Nick thinks the world of her and why he's so attentive and considerate, but. . . ."

Mother gave a deep sigh. "Don't tell me you've come up with another excuse."

"Call it an excuse if you want to. Nick's mother was nice to me, but I knew right away she'd never accept me. She doesn't like me because I'm not Italian and I'm not Catholic."

"I'll call it another excuse," Mother said. "What matters is how Nick feels about you—not his mother."

Tracey thought of Bianca's sister-in-law. She almost told Mother she'd never stand for being treated like an outsider by Nick's mother. She almost said she wanted a mother-in-law who'd welcome her with open arms and accept her for who she was. But saying this would be admitting to Mother that she'd thought about marriage. She'd barely admitted it to herself.

"I'm going to get dressed for church," she said.

When she returned from church, she found Mother in the den. Sections of the *New York Times* and the *Staten Island Advance* were strewn all over the couch and floor.

"Nita's picture's in the *Advance*," she said. "It's here somewhere." She began to rummage through the scattered pages.

She seemed somewhat subdued, Tracey thought.

Was it because of their earlier argument? She was about to tell her she was sorry for being short with her when she noticed the *Times* business section lying on the floor. On the first page, under a prominent headline, she saw a photo of Dad.

Mother saw her looking down at it. "Your father's putting up another tower," she said.

Tracey picked up the paper. "Then you've read this, Mom?" she asked.

"I glanced through it," she replied. "There's another photo in the *Advance* and an article mentioning he was once a resident of Staten Island." She handed Tracey the *Advance*'s business section. "Local boy makes good," she said with a wry smile.

Tracey sat down and read the article in the Staten Island paper. It was more of a personal profile than the *Times* ran. It included a description of Dad's lodge on the Maine coast and not only mentioned he used to live on Staten Island but specified he lived in Grymes Hill.

"Everyone we knew will read this article today and remember how he walked out on me," Mother said.

There was no use telling her nobody else except the attorneys knew it was Dad who wanted the divorce. Mother's bitterness made her imagine everyone knew.

"What time is Nick coming for you?" Mother asked.

"In about an hour. I guess I'd better get changed."

"Do you want something to eat before you go?"

"Thanks, Mom, but Nick said his mother will pack something for us to eat on the boat."

"This is the mother you say doesn't like you?"

"Don't start that again, Mom," Tracey said.

She was in her bedroom when she heard Nick's truck in the drive. Looking out, she watched him walk to the door.

She gave an inward sigh. Telling herself she'd gotten as close to the "L" word as she should had seemed a lot simpler this morning. Seeing him aroused strong thoughts of last night and the kissing bench. She wanted to know that sweet ardor again.

When she went downstairs, she found Mother and Nick talking and laughing. *Nick always brought out the best in Mother,* she thought. They liked one another. A feeling of regret came over her. It could never be this way between Nick's mother and her.

"It's a great day for a sail," she said as Nick turned the truck out of the drive.

"Right. There's just enough breeze to make it interesting," he replied. "Have you done much sailing?"

"I've only been on a sailboat three or four times in my entire life," she said with a laugh.

"Is that right?" he asked, surprised. "I haven't done much more than that myself, but I thought you'd be an old hand at it."

"Why would you think that?"

"It's just an impression I have of you."

"How did you get that impression? We've never talked about sailing. The subject never came up till your friend invited us out on his boat."

"I read an article in the *Advance* this morning about the business tycoon Martin G. Wood," he replied. "It said he used to live on Grymes Hill. I put two and two together. He's your father, isn't he?"

"Yes," she replied. "But what's that got to do with me being an old hand at sailing?"

"The article described a lodge on the coast of Maine and somehow I pictured you in your own sailboat."

She laughed. "Well, you'll find out today how little I know about it. I just hope I don't fall overboard."

"If you do, I'll dive in and rescue you," he said.

Knowing she was the daughter of Martin G. Wood must have startled him, she thought, but his usual easy banter told her it hadn't made her see her in a different light. She recalled the changed attitudes of several college classmates when they found out. Some decided she must be a snob and took an instant disliking to her. Others started showering her with sudden attention.

They found Nick's friends waiting at the marina. Tracey liked the boat's owner, Jim, and his girlfriend, Rebecca, right away. She sensed the feeling was mutual. By the time they'd sailed out of Great Kills

Harbor into open water, she'd decided to invite them
to the pool party.

It would be nice for Nick to have some of his
friends there, too. She wanted to get to know Nick's
other friends, too. Abruptly, she cut off that last
thought. It sounded too much as if their relationship
was going to progress. With his mother prejudiced
against her, she knew it couldn't.

They sailed around Sandy Hook, and into the Na-
vesink River. Tracey and Rebecca relaxed and talked
while the men handled the sails and tiller.

Nick opened the cooler he'd brought from home.
"Let's see what my mother put in here," he said. "She
told me it was going to be a little snack."

The little snack turned out to be meatball sandwiches with Italian sausage sauce, individual contain-
ers of pasta salad and an assortment of pastry and
cookies.

"My mother never saw anyone she didn't want to
feed," Nick said.

Tracey thought about all the family members Mrs.
Ferrone fed every day—not only fed, but nurtured.
She was a caring person and she'd passed the trait
along to Nick. It would be easy to like Mrs. Ferrone,
but Mrs Ferrone would never like her. She wanted an
Italian Catholic girl for Nick, and nothing could
change that.

After they docked into the marina, they stayed

aboard awhile and talked. Tracey invited Rebecca and Jim to the pool party.

"Next Sunday at four o'clock, rain or shine," she said. "If the weather doesn't cooperate, we'll move indoors."

They seemed delighted. "Thanks. We'll be there," Jim said.

Tracey glanced at Nick. The look on his face told her he was pleased.

Mother was out when they got back to the house. They went to the poolside and sat on the kissing bench until they heard the Blue Bomb in the drive.

Tracey smoothed her hair before they went into the house.

As usual, he and mother greeted each other with a hug and kiss. They sat in the den and told her about the sail.

"Tracey was nice enough to invite my friends to the pool party." Nick said.

"The more the merrier," Mother said. "Your friends are our friends, Nick."

She asked him to stay and have dinner with them.

"I wish I could, but I should be heading home," he said.

He didn't need to say why, Tracey thought. She knew he wanted to give his mother a break. The thought didn't stir her to the mean conclusions it once did. Mother was right. He was a good son.

She tried not to think of what else Mother had said. *"Good sons make good husbands."*

Chapter Thirteen

It seemed strange not to meet Nita on the 8:10 ferry the next morning. But if she were here, she'd be asking questions about Nick, and it would be difficult to ignore them. He was in her thoughts so consistently, she felt she had to talk about him.

Bianca came into her office just before noon. "Are you free for lunch?" she asked. "I have to talk to you." She seemed subdued.

"Sure," Tracey replied. She glanced at her watch. "Shall we go now?"

They went to the same restaurant where they'd lunched two weeks ago. *So much had happened since then,* Tracey thought. In spite of all her negative thoughts about Nick and his mother, she and Nick had grown closer with every passing day. She knew that Nick was nothing like Bianca's brother. She hoped Bianca wouldn't bring the subject up.

But today Bianca's mind seemed set strictly on trouble with the current man in her life.

"I'm afraid it's over, Tracey," she said, her mascara growing moist. "I'm heartbroken. There'll never be another man like him."

Tracey suppressed a smile. "How many times have you told me that?"

"I know I thought I was in love a few times, but when we split up I never felt like this. I feel so depressed. I'm afraid I won't be able to play a good Emerald Drake."

"I thought you were getting along so well with this one," Tracey said. "What happened?"

"We were at a party, and he got jealous because I was being pleasant to another man."

"Just how pleasant were you being?" Tracey asked.

"We had a few laughs while we were dancing."

"That's all?"

"Well, maybe he was holding me a little close. Anyway, Eddie was furious. After he took me home we had a terrible fight. He told me I'd made a spectacle of myself and humiliated him. I told him if he was going to be jealous every time I was having a good time, he could hit the road. He stormed out of my apartment and I haven't seen or heard from him since."

"When did this happen?"

"Saturday night. Oh, Tracey, what am I going to do?"

"Have you thought of phoning him and saying you're sorry?"

"I know he'd hang up the minute he heard my voice."

"Give him a chance to cool down. If he hasn't called you by the weekend, call him."

"If he doesn't call me by the weekend, then I'll know he's through with me and there'd be no use calling him. Oh, Tracey, I can't stand it. I'll be all alone over the weekend."

"I just thought of something," Tracey said. "If he hasn't phoned you by Saturday, why don't you come out to Staten Island and stay over until Monday? I'm having a pool party Sunday night. You could have a good time and forget your troubles."

Bianca's woebegone face lit up. "A pool party? Oh that sounds like fun."

"Give me a call and let me know," Tracey said. "I could pick you up at the ferry Saturday, afternoon. We could go in to the studios together on Monday morning."

Bianca's face was all smiles now. "Thanks a million, Tracey. Will there be any extra men at your party? I just bought a new bikini."

"I'll try and round up a few spares," Tracey said with a laugh. "And maybe Nick can get you a date for Saturday night."

"Nick? The Italian Stallion? How's it going with you two? Have you met his mother yet?"

"I met her over the weekend," Tracey replied.

Bianca seemed to forget her own troubles. "And was I right when I told you she's just like my mother?"

"Not exactly," Tracey replied. "I found out she's a remarkable woman."

Bianca stared at her. "Remarkable? How?"

Tracey told her about Mrs. Ferrone's devoted care for Nick's father, grandparents and Aunt Tessie. "She didn't fake that fainting spell. The poor woman had been going full blast since early morning doing housework and planning her daughter's wedding, in addition to caring for four ailing family members. She was exhausted that night."

Bianca looked doubtful. "But she still has Nick under her thumb, doesn't she? He's a mama's boy, isn't he, just like my brother?"

Tracey shook her head. "No, he's not a mama's boy. He's caring and considerate because he's knows how much she does for her family."

Bianca cast her a probing look. "But there's something else, isn't there? Everything isn't all sweetness and light, is it?"

"Yes, there's something else," Tracey said with a sigh. "Nick's mother is like yours in one way. She'll never accept me."

Bianca nodded her head. "She wants an Italian Catholic girl for her Nicky."

"Yes. Of course nothing was said. She was nice to

me, but there was no mistaking the vibes. She doesn't like me."

"Have you talked about this with Nick?"

"Oh, no. We're nowhere near that stage yet," Tracey replied. But she knew they were. It wouldn't take many more tête-à-têtes on the kissing bench before he'd bring up the subject of a commitment. What would she say when he did? And Bianca thought *she* had man trouble!

"So the woman is another Mother Theresa. She still has some nerve not accepting you," Bianca said. "You're a great gal, Tracey. She should be thrilled you're interested in Nick. He could have brought some chippy home for her to meet."

"Thanks, but if the chippy met the right ethnic and church requirements, she'd probably prefer her to me," Tracey replied.

When they said goodbye at the elevators, Bianca seemed more interested in a visit to Staten Island than a phone call from her jealous boyfriend. "I'll let you know what boat I'm taking on Saturday," she said.

When Tracey arrived home that evening, the Blue Bomb was in the garage, but Mother wasn't anywhere, to be found. She wanted to tell her about Bianca coming Saturday and staying overnight to attend the pool party.

"Mom, I'm home. Where are you?" she called. There was no response.

She opened the basement door and called again. "Mom, are you down there?" Still no response.

If Mother were in her bedroom, she would have heard her calling. Maybe she was taking a shower, she thought. On the way upstairs she glanced out the window at the pool area to make sure she wasn't there.

When she got to the upstairs hall she saw Mother's bedroom door was closed. Mother wasn't one to take naps. Tracey knocked on the door. "Mom, may I come in?"

"Yes, come in dear," came the reply.

She entered the bedroom, dimmed by drapes pulled over the windows. She saw Mother on the bed, wearing her bathrobe. "Are you just out of the shower, Mom?" she asked. "I called when I came in. Why are the drapes drawn?" She stepped over to the window and pulled them back. Light flooded the room. When she turned around she saw the hem of Mother's nightgown protruding from beneath her robe.

A startling suspicion flashed into her mind. Mother had been up here since morning. She hadn't even dressed.

"Are you sick, Mom?" she asked, sitting on the edge of the bed.

Mother shook her head. "I'm okay. I was just resting."

Tracey had never known Mother to take a nap during the day. Again, the nightgown made her think she might have been in her bedroom since early morning.

Mother sat up and swung her legs over the side of the bed. "I had no idea it was so late."

Had she eaten anything since morning? Tracey wondered.

"Mom, I'm going to bring you up a glass of iced tea and then I'm going to fix us some dinner," she said.

"You don't have to do that, dear. I'll be down in the kitchen in a few minutes."

Tracey knew it was signal for her to leave. "See you downstairs, Mom," she said. She went down to the kitchen and started to make iced tea.

A few minutes later, Mother appeared, fully dressed.

"How was your day, dear?" she asked. Tracey detected a note of false cheerfulness in her voice.

"Fine." She wanted to ask her the same question, but it was obvious something was wrong. She couldn't imagine what it was.

As they prepared dinner, Mother barely spoke a word. Tracey's concern grew. She'd read about depression and this seemed to fit right in with the symptoms. She decided to give their family doctor a call after dinner. In the meantime, she'd try and cheer Mother up with light talk.

"I missed seeing Nita on the 8:10," she said. "I suppose she and Don are having a wonderful time.

Where's that picture of her you said was in the *Advance?* I want to clip it for my scrapbook."

"I clipped it for you last night," Mother said. "It's on the coffee table in the den."

When they sat down to eat, Mother seemed to perk up a bit. "Forgive me for being such poor company tonight, dear. I've had the blues ever since you left for work this morning."

"What brought this mood on?" Tracey asked.

"Oh, I know it's silly of me, but I got to reminiscing, and the next thing I knew I was bawling like a baby. I called the office and left word I wouldn't be in today, but to call me if something important came up. Fortunately it didn't. I wouldn't have been able to sell a fur hat in Russia."

"What were you reminiscing about?" Tracey asked. She suspected it had to do with happier days when the Blue Bomb was the Blue Streak.

She wasn't far off the mark. "I got to thinking about the wonderful life we had when you were a child, the fun we had on family vacations," Mother said. "And I thought about you and Nita when you were children and how we often took her along on family outings. And I thought about her getting married and I prayed her husband would always love her."

Bittersweet memories, Tracey thought.

"And I thought about you, dear, and the wonderful young man who's come into your life, and I prayed you'd fall in love with him because I know he loves you and he'll never forsake you."

She paused, looking into Tracey's eyes. "I feel in my heart that Nick is the kind of man who'll love you as long as he lives."

It was at that moment that Tracey remembered today was Mother and Dad's wedding anniversary. They would have been married twenty-six years.

Never before had Mother seemed depressed on the anniversary. Though Tracey usually remembered the day, she didn't mention it to Mother, and Mother never said anything about it. It was part of another life.

Mother's words resounded in her mind. *"I prayed Nita's husband would always love her . . . Nick is the kind of man who'll love you as long as he lives."*

She longed to let Mother know what Dad had told her. He hadn't left because he'd stopped loving her. She wanted to tell Mother that, even as he went out the door, he still loved her and would have turned around and come back if he could be sure she'd never denigrate him again.

But there was no telling what Mother's reaction would be if she knew her incessant needling had driven Dad away. The shock might put her into a worse state of mind than she'd been in today.

She decided to talk it over with Nick when he came to the house tonight. Maybe he could help her decide what to do.

By the time Nick arrived, Mother had worked her-self out of her blues. There was no trace of her earlier mood when she greeted Nick with the usual hug.

"I can't stay long," Nick told them. "I'm getting up at the crack of dawn tomorrow. As a special favor to one of my best customers, I'm starting to work early on his car so he'll have it in time to go on a trip tomorrow afternoon."

Mother took her cue from this. "I think I'll go up to my room and read awhile," she said. She'd barely reached the top of the stairway when Nick gathered Tracey into his arms.

"I have something to discuss with you," she said, after two breathtaking kisses. "We talked about it be-fore."

"It's about whether or not to tell your mother about what your father told you, isn't it?" he asked.

"What are you, a mind reader?"

"I'm more of a heart reader. I can tell when some-thing's weighing heavily on your heart," he said.

She told him about Mother's blue spell and its con-nection to the anniversary and Nita's wedding—ev-erything except what she'd said about Nick.

"Today being their anniversary, she was thinking about the years when she and Dad were in love. She thinks he wanted a divorce because he didn't love her anymore. How do you think she'd react if she knew

Dad still loved her when he left, and that his reason for leaving was her own doing?" Tracey asked.

"I told you before, I think you ought to tell her. She has the right to know," he said. "But she's your mother, and I think you know better than I how she might react."

"I'm afraid of making a mistake," she said.

"Letting someone know the truth is usually no mistake," he said. "I should think, after all these years of believing he'd fallen out of love with her, she'd be comforted to know he hadn't. Take your time, Tracey. I know when you make your decision it'll be the right one."

After he'd gone home, she realized she hadn't told either Nick or Mother about Bianca's visit. It didn't matter, she thought. Knowing Bianca, she could have made up with her jealous boyfriend before the weekend, or even have a new man in her life. In either case, she wouldn't be coming to Staten Island.

She turned her thoughts back to the question of telling Mother the truth about the divorce.

Chapter Fourteen

Two days went by without Tracey making a decision. But there was no hurry, she thought. As Nick had advised, she'd take her time.

Meanwhile, Mother was back to her old self, planning Sunday's party. She'd engaged a caterer to provide and serve the food, and she'd bought some new poolside furniture. She was pleased when Tracey told her Bianca might come.

"Unless you invite more people, the head count is at thirty-one," she announced.

When Nick dropped in Wednesday night, he told Tracey his sister Estelle wanted to meet her. "She's the one who was out when you met the rest of the family," he said. "I told her I'd asked you to come to her wedding and she asked if I would bring you over tomorrow night after dinner."

"Great. I want to meet her, too," Tracey said.

* * *

The Ferrone living room looked almost empty when Nick took Tracey there Thursday night. Nick's grandparents were not present. Neither were his two younger sisters. Estelle, Aunt Tessie and Mrs. Ferrone greeted them. His father, in a corner of the room in his wheelchair, acknowledged her as best he could. Tracey noticed he didn't smile at her as he had the other day. Was it her imagination, or did he, too, seem cold?

But Estelle's manner was friendly. "I just had to see the reason Nick's never home anymore," she said when Nick introduced them.

Tracey liked her at once. She exuded all the warmth Tracey wished she could get from Mrs. Ferrone, who sent out vibes even chillier than before.

Aunt Tessie seemed somewhat friendlier, though Tracey sensed a slight antagonism in her manner as well. But both she and Mrs. Ferrone warmed up enough to ask Tracey about her job.

"Nick says you're a producer on that show, 'Road of Life,' " Aunt Tessie said. "He said you're friends with the actress who plays Emerald. That's our favorite soap, isn't it, Gena?"

Mrs. Ferrone nodded. "We watch it every day. That Emerald, she's man-crazy."

"Do you know what's going to happen?" Aunt Tessie asked. "Is she going to get Brent away from his wife?"

"I don't think that's been decided yet," Tracey replied. "The writers are still working on it."

"That home-wrecker, I hope the writers have something bad to happen to her," Mrs. Ferrone said.

Nick laughed. "Come on. Ma, you know you and Aunt Tessie would miss Emerald if she wasn't on the show anymore."

"I don't want her killed off," Mrs. Ferrone said. "But she's got to be stopped before she steals every husband on the show."

"Maybe she could go blind," Aunt Tessie added. "That way she couldn't see the men."

Mrs. Ferrone gave a hearty laugh. Tracey laughed, too. "I'll suggest that to the writers," she said.

For those few minutes, Tracey sensed the lessening of Mrs. Ferrone's antagonism. She could almost imagine how it could be—she and Nick's mother laughing together as friends united in their feelings for Nick.

But the respite was brief. Mrs. Ferrone got right back to the forced friendliness and the cold vibes.

Aunt Tessie helped her serve coffee and a large assortment of pastries. Mrs. Ferrone had to answer several calls from the grandparents upstairs. Her frequent absences from the room relieved Tracey's tension. The aura of hostility seemed to get stronger every minute.

Nick seemed unaware of the antagonism. Every time she glanced at him, he'd glance back with a broad smile.

She could not decide whether or not Estelle knew.

With her wedding day approaching, she probably couldn't think of anything else.

If it hadn't been for the short discussion of Bianca's role on the show, the visit would have been unbearable, Tracey thought. Suddenly, an idea struck her. If Bianca came to Staten Island on Saturday, she'd take her to meet Mrs. Ferrone and Aunt Tessie.

Emerald Drake had made a small break in the ice. Maybe meeting the actress who played her could shatter it. She felt an overwhelming need to be friends with Nick's mother. Once they were friends, maybe her not being Italian or Catholic wouldn't matter so much. It was worth a try, she thought, but first she had to be sure Bianca hadn't made up with her boyfriend.

This thought sustained her throughout the rest of the visit.

On the way home she told Nick about her idea, but not her reason.

"Great," he said. "When will you know if she's coming?"

"Sometime Saturday."

"Okay. I won't tell Mother and Aunt Tessie till we know for sure."

He had no idea how much she was counting on her idea. She wondered how he could be unaware of his mother's antagonism.

Bianca phoned Saturday morning. "I'm making the three o'clock boat," she said. She sounded upbeat. No mention of the man who'd broken her heart.

Tracey phoned Nick at his shop and told him.

"Great," he said. "I'll call home and let Mother know she and Aunt Tessie are about to meet the sultry siren."

Later, he called back. "Mom's all excited. She wants to have you and Bianca over for dinner tonight. Okay?"

This might be the breakthrough she'd hoped for, Tracey thought. "That was very nice of your mother," she said.

"And I got a date for Bianca with my cousin Johnny DeLucca," he added. "He'll be there for dinner, too. He's a good-looking guy, full of fun."

If he was anything like Nick, Bianca would go for him, Tracey thought.

"This is wonderful of you," Bianca said when Tracey picked her up at the ferry. "Being alone on a weekend is death. Did your Italian Stallion get a date for me?"

"Yes, he got his cousin Johnny DeLucca. I've never met him, but Nick says he's good-looking. Nick's mother has invited us all over for dinner tonight. She and Nick's aunt watch the show regularly and they're all excited about meeting Emerald."

Bianca's face lighted up at the mention of Nick's cousin, but when she heard about dinner with Nick's mother she frowned. "The way Nick's mama treats you, I'm surprised you'd want to do anything to please the old girl."

"She's nice to me, but she isn't friendly," Tracey said. "I thought it might help if I arranged for her to meet her favorite soap opera character."

"You think that's going to make her accept you? Not a chance. She has some nerve, letting you do this for her when all the time she'd like you to get lost."

Mother was out doing errands when they got to the house. Tracey showed Bianca to the guest room and put her suitcase on the luggage rack at the foot of the four-poster bed.

"This is some layout you've got here," Bianca said, peering into the guest bath. "You told me you had a big house with a swimming pool, but I didn't know it was going to be like this."

"I'll show you the pool," Tracey said.

Everything was ready for tomorrow's party. The gardener had hauled away the last of the storm's debris and replaced or replanted damaged shrubs and plants. The pool maintenance crew had finished their work and the water sparkled in the afternoon sunshine. Mother had arranged the new outdoor furniture around the poolside. Tracey felt her heart sink for a moment. She thought Mother had thrown away the kissing bench. But she spied it in a far corner of the pool area, in the shade of a small tree.

"I'd like to live like this," Bianca said. "And some-day I will, even if I have to marry into money."

"You'll make it on your own," Tracey said. "You're a good actress, Bianca."

Mother's voice sounded from the house. "Tracey. Where are you, dear?"

"We're out by the pool, Mom," she called back.

A moment later Mother appeared. She'd been out getting last-minute things for the party, she said. She greeted Bianca in her usual gracious manner.

"What time are you going to Nick's house?" she asked.

"He's coming for us at six," Tracey said. A ripple of anticipation went through her heart. It happened every time she thought of seeing him again.

When Tracey and Bianca went upstairs to change clothes, Bianca had more uncomplimentary things to say about Nick's mother. "Who does that Mama Ferrone think she is? She should be thankful someone with your background even gave Nick a second glance."

Nick came for them in his mother's car. "Emerald Drake would never ride in a truck," he said.

Tracey was glad to note he and Bianca seemed congenial from the moment of their introduction.

"Johnny's meeting us at the house," he said. "You'll like him, Bianca, and if he doesn't like you he's crazy."

Tracey noticed Bianca's eyes appraising Nick. On the way out to the car, she whispered to Tracey, "If this Johnny's anything like Nick, I'll take him."

Aunt Tessie greeted them at the door, bursting with excitement. After Tracey introduced her to Bianca, she ushered them into the living room where family members had gathered. They were all there except Nick's sisters and his mother. "The girls had dates and Gena's in the kitchen," Aunt Tessie said.

She introduced Bianca. "She's a big television star." she said. Tracey noticed she couldn't keep her eyes off Bianca.

Nick's cousin was a nice-looking young man. Tracey made sure Bianca was seated next to him before she told Nick she'd go out to the kitchen and help his mother.

"Good luck," he said with a grin. "She doesn't like anyone in the kitchen when she's cooking."

As she walked through the dining room, she noticed the table set with a white linen cloth and napkins and newly polished silver. The half-empty walnut china cabinet indicated Mrs. Ferrone had taken out her good dishes for the occasion.

She stepped into the big kitchen, where Nick's mother was basting a roast.

"Hello, Mrs. Ferrone. Tell me what I can do to help," she said.

Mrs. Ferrone brushed a lock of hair away from her face. "Thank you for offering, but it's almost ready."

"Can I carry the dishes to the table?"

"You don't need to do that. Go back in the front room with the others. I'll be in to meet your friend the actress in a few minutes."

Tracey left the kitchen with a sinking heart. Her plan to win Mrs. Ferrone over was not off to a good start.

In the living room, Nick smiled at her. "What did I tell you?" he asked. "When Mother puts on a meal, it's a one-woman show."

His mother appeared a few minutes later. She'd taken off her apron and smoothed her hair.

Tracey could sense her excitement as she was introduced to Bianca. "I'm pleased to meet you, Miss Morelli," she said. "I watch your show every day, and I'm always glad when it's an episode with you in it."

"Thanks," Bianca said. "So you're the mother of this big hunk of man." She rolled her eyes at Nick.

Mrs. Ferrone looked startled for a moment. "Well, dinner's ready," she said. "Come to the table, everyone."

Nick wheeled his father into the dining room. Grandma and Aunt Tessie guided Grandpa. Bianca sat down between Johnny and Nick, with Tracey on Nick's other side.

Tracey noticed goblets at each place, and a glass decanter with red wine.

"Dominick, will you make a toast to our guest, Miss Morelli?" Mrs. Ferrone said.

Nick rose, glass in hand. "To Emerald Drake," he said. "Long may she reign as a soap opera queen."

"Hey. That's not bad, Nicky," Bianca said. She picked up her goblet and took a generous quaff. "And this stuff's not bad either."

Accustomed as she was to Bianca's way of expressing herself, this was a bit too breezy, Tracey thought.

Mrs. Ferrone heaped everyone's plate with meat and gravy and potatoes and vegetables. Hot garlic bread was passed around. Salads bowls were filled.

"How about hitting my glass again, Nicky?" Bianca said. As she handed him her goblet, Tracey saw her flutter her eyes at him.

"Is there something else you'd like, Miss Morelli?" Nick's mother asked.

"No, thanks. And you can forget the Morelli and call me Bianca."

"All right, Bianca," Mrs. Ferrone replied.

"As a matter of fact, I'm going to forget the Morelli myself," Bianca continued. "I've decided to cut off the 'i' and be Bianca Morrell. It has a classier sound to it."

Tracey squirmed with embarrassment. Bianca should have known better than to make such a statement. The wine had loosened her tongue, she decided.

Grandma looked at Nick's mother. "Sounds to me like she's ashamed of being Italian," she said.

Bianca glared at her. "You talking about me?"

Nick cleared his throat. "Ma, could I have some more meat, please? You outdid yourself on the roast today. Anyone for seconds on the meat? How about you, Johnny?"

"Sure, I'll have a little more," Johnny replied.

But Grandma would not be diverted. "I don't see anyone else at this table who wants to change her name."

"That's enough, Mama," Mrs. Ferrone said as she heaped Nick's plate with meat and gravy. "I'm sure our guest meant no offense."

Tracey heard Nick's whisper. "I don't think this is going as well as we thought it would."

"Don't give Bianca any more wine," she whispered back.

"So, Bianca, are you from New York or from some other city?" Nick's mother asked. She was making a valiant attempt to cover the exchange between Grandma and Bianca, Tracey thought.

"I'm from Pittsburgh," Bianca replied. "My parents still live there."

Parents? Tracey thought. Hadn't Bianca mentioned her mother was a widow?

"They must be very proud of you," Aunt Tessie said. "Not everybody has a daughter on a soap opera."

"Do you have sisters or brothers?" Mrs. Ferrone asked.

"No, my parents just had me," Bianca replied.

Tracey felt a jolt of surprise. What about the mama's boy brother? She couldn't imagine why Bianca had invented a whole new family for herself, but at least it was a safe topic.

Looking at Nick, she whispered, "The talk's going better."

He nodded and smiled, but suddenly his smile faded and a strange expression crossed his face.

"What's the matter? she asked.

He whispered back. "Bianca's playing footsie with me."

Tracey tried to choke back her laughter. She glanced at Nick's mother to see if she'd noticed the suppressed chuckles.

But Mrs. Ferrone's gaze was fixed on Bianca. "What are your parents' occupations?" she asked.

Tracey forgot the footsie incident for a moment as she imagined what professions Bianca might invent for her newly fabricated parents. Would her father be an astronaut and her mother a brain surgeon?

"My father's a priest and my mother's a nun," Bianca said.

Grandma stood up. "I've heard enough of this," she announced. "I'll eat my dessert in the kitchen." With that, she grabbed her cane and hobbled out of the room.

"Can't you take a joke?" Bianca called after her. "I'll bet I'm just as good a Catholic as you are."

Tracey looked at Nick. "If I ever get an idea like

this again, please stop me," she whispered. Never had she been so embarrassed.

They managed to get through the remainder of the meal without disruption.

Once or twice Tracey caught Mrs. Ferrone staring at Bianca. She couldn't see if Bianca noticed because Nick's broad shoulders blocked her view of Bianca's face.

"We'll have coffee in the living room," Mrs. Ferrone said. They all left the table except Mrs. Ferrone, who stayed behind to clear away the dishes. Tracey wanted to help her, but she'd been rebuffed once and didn't want it to happen again.

In the living room, Bianca squeezed herself next to Nick on the sofa instead of sitting next to Tracey where there was plenty of room. By now Tracey felt sure Bianca was making a play for Nick. Poor Johnny—she'd ignored him all evening.

Mrs. Ferrone came into the living room. "Tracey," she said, "I need your help with the coffee."

Tracey sprang to her feet and followed her into the kitchen.

There, Mrs. Ferrone made sure nobody was within earshot before saying, "I want to warn you about your friend Bianca. Believe me, she's no friend. I noticed how she batted her eyes at Nick and how she slunk down in her chair in the dining room. I wasn't born yesterday. I know what she was up to. Trying to play footsie with him, that's what."

She'd called him Nick, not Dominick. As Tracey stared at her in surprise, she continued, "She's just like that slut she plays on the show and she's out to get our Nick."

Our Nick! Tracey felt her heart leap.

"I noticed it, too, Mrs. Ferrone," she said. "What do you think I should do about it?"

"I'd load her onto the ferry and send her back to Manhattan as soon as possible. Not that I think she'd be any threat to a nice girl like you, but with men, you never know."

Suddenly, she broke into a laugh. "Her father a priest and her mother a nun! If she hadn't behaved like a hussy, I'd have told her it was funny."

She loaded a tray with cups and saucers, a sugar bowl and a creamer. "Take these in. I'll bring the coffeepot."

Half an hour later, Nick told Tracey they should be going soon. "But I want to help your mother clean up the kitchen," she said.

His mother must have overheard. "Tessie will help me," she said. "You run along. Remember what I told you about putting that baggage on the boat."

Chapter Fifteen

On the way to Tracey's house, Nick and Johnny hardly spoke a word. *Not surprising,* Tracey thought. *Johnny must feel as if Bianca didn't like him; she'd ignored him all evening, and Nick must feel as if she liked him too much.* As for herself, she didn't know how to handle this. She knew there was no danger of losing Nick to Bianca, but she was annoyed with her for her behavior tonight.

Bianca, too, was quiet. Tracey had expected her to leap into the front seat with Nick, but she'd made no attempt. She got in back with Johnny.

As they turned into the drive, Tracey saw a light from Mother's bedroom window. "I guess Mother's going to hit the sack early," she said. "I suppose I should, too. We have a lot to do before the party to-morrow."

"I'll come up after lunch and help," Nick said. He

glanced into the rearview mirror. "Johnny and Bianca are getting along better," he said.

They said goodnight at the front door with a fleeting kiss. With Bianca and Johnny close by, it was the best they could do.

She and Bianca hadn't been inside for more than a moment before Bianca began to laugh. "I think it worked," she said.

"What are you talking about, Bianca?" Tracey asked.

"Bianca looked at her in surprise. "Don't tell me you fell for my Emerald Drake routine. Didn't you know it was all an act to make Mama Ferrone appreciate you?"

"You were putting on an act the whole time? Oh, Bianca, your performance was worthy of an Oscar. And you're right, it worked. While we were in the kitchen, Nick's mother told me I should put you on the next boat to Manhattan so you wouldn't steal Nick away from me."

Bianca's face suddenly sobered. "How are you going to explain this to Nick? I'm almost afraid to tell you, but at the table I—"

"I know," Tracey said. "Nick told me, and so did his mother. She saw you slink down in your chair and bat your eyes at him. I'll tell Nick it was the wine. Someday I'll tell him the whole story."

She realized she'd said "someday" as if they might have a future together.

"I told Johnny I was sorry," Bianca said. "I let him think I'd had too much wine. Will he be at the party tomorrow?"

"I asked him and he said he'd try and make it. Now that you two are getting along, I think he'll come."

"I hope he does. He's a nice guy. I'd like to know him better."

"Excuse me for asking," Tracey said, "but what about Eddie?"

"Eddie who?" Bianca replied.

Tracey skipped church the next day to help Mother with party preparations. Bianca helped, too.

Nick arrived around noon. "It looks like you haven't left anything for me to do," he said. She noticed he didn't seem uneasy around Bianca. Later, he told her Johnny had explained she'd had too much wine. "Johnny's coming to the party," he said. "He likes her and wants to see her again."

"That's good," Tracey said. She hoped Bianca had finally reached the end of the trail of broken hearts and there would never be a "Johnny who?"

"You look radiant today," Nick told her.

"I feel radiant," she said. How she longed to tell him she'd achieved a breakthrough with his mother. But how could she when he was unaware of the previous situation? "Your mother put on a lovely dinner last night," she said.

"You made a hit with her," he said. "I couldn't believe it when she asked you to help her in the kitchen."

She still had a way to go with his mother, she thought. What was the old saying? One wave does not an ocean make—or something like that.

"She wants you to come over after dinner tomorrow night," Nick said. "She has something to talk to you about."

A tiny barb of apprehension plucked at her heart. Was Nick's mother going to tell she liked her but she hoped when Nick got serious it would be with an Italian Catholic girl?

At the party, Nita was almost as thrilled to meet Bianca as she was to be the guest of honor with her new husband. She was also also excited over the possibility of a romance between Tracey and Nick. Tracey was attempting to downplay this, when she suddenly realized she hadn't seen Mother for quite awhile.

Remembering the night she'd come home and couldn't find her, she began to worry. "She wouldn't leave the party without saying good night," she told Nick. "Where could she be?"

"I'll look around at the other end of the pool," Nick said. Tracey searched the area near the house.

"Have you seen Mother?" she asked a bikini-clad Bianca, talking with Johnny near the barbecue grill.

"I saw her go into the house about half an hour ago," Bianca replied.

With her apprehension growing, Tracey went into the house and up to Mother's bedroom. There, she found Mother curled up on the window seat, looking down at the party.

"Are you okay, Mom?" she asked.

"Yes, I'm all right. Just another case of the blues," Mother replied. I was having such a good time, when all of a sudden I began to reminisce again."

Tracey sat down beside her. "About the pool parties you and Dad used to have with your friends?"

She nodded. "Yes. Tonight brought it all back. Oh Tracey, why did it have to happen? Why couldn't your father have stayed in love with me?"

At that moment, Tracey made her decision. She must tell Mother that Dad still loved her when he left. If she didn't, she might have these blue spells the rest of her life.

"Mom" she said. "I had lunch with Dad last week and he told me something you should know. . . ."

She watched Mother's face as she relayed everything Dad had told her. She watched it go from a look of surprise to a look of anguish. Her eyes filled with tears. She covered her face with her hands, got up from the window seat and ran into her bathroom.

Tracey felt her heart turn into a lump of lead. What had she expected? Had she truly believed she'd see any joy on Mother's face? She went to the bathroom door and knocked. There was no response. She turned the knob. The door was locked.

She ran down the stairs and into the pool area, look-ing for Nick. When she found him she was almost in tears herself. She told him what had happened. With-out hesitation, he took her by the hand and they ran into the house and up to Mother's room. The bathroom door was still locked.

"Mrs. Wood . . . Christine," Nick called. "Will you open the door?"

A wave of relief swept over Tracey as she heard the lock being released. A moment later Mother opened the door.

Tracey expected to see a sad, tear-stained face. In-stead, there was no trace of her earlier tears. Her eyes stared at them with an almost-blank expression.

"Mom, we were worried about you," Tracey said.

Mother didn't reply, but brushed past them into her room. "I'm going to bed," she said. "Good night."

"It's only half past seven," Nick said. "Don't you want to come down and join the party?"

Mother shook her head.

"Okay," Nick said. He motioned for Tracey to leave and followed her out into the hall, closing the door behind him.

"Should we leave her alone like that?" Tracey asked, casting a fearful glance over her shoulder.

"She wouldn't have come out of the bathroom if she wasn't feeling a little better," Nick said.

"You were the one who got her to come out," Tracey replied. "She has a special feeling for you. Do you think she'll be all right?"

"It must have been a shock, finding out the truth after all these years, but, yes, I think she'll be all right. If she isn't herself in the morning, it would be a good idea to call your family doctor."

"I shouldn't have told her."

"Don't go blaming yourself, Tracey. You've both carried this around long enough. Now let's go back to the party. I'll go up and check on her in a little while."

For Tracey, the party was over. She settled herself in a poolside chair, her mind a jumble of regrets.

Bianca came over and sat down beside her. "Is something wrong?" she asked.

"Mother's not feeling well," Tracey replied. She couldn't bring herself to tell her the whole story.

"Then we should start calling it quits on the party," Bianca said. "Everyone has had enough to eat and drink and everyone's out of the pool. I think this is a good time to start winding down."

Tracey looked across the pool, where couples were dancing to stereo music. "But they've only just started dancing," she said.

"They'll have a little more time before it starts clearing out," Bianca replied. "Where's Nick?"

"He just went up to look in on Mother."

"When he comes back, tell him what I said. Johnny and I will circulate and drop some hints that it's time to break it up."

When Nick returned he reported Mother was in bed, reading.

"Bianca thinks we should end the party," Tracey said.

"She's right. And the quickest way to end a party is to close the bar and turn off the music."

"I hate to do that. It seems so abrupt. Bianca and Johnny are going around dropping hints.

"Good. If a few people take the hint and start leaving, others will notice and get the idea."

"Did you talk to Mother at all?"

"Not really. I just asked her how she was doing and she said fine. I think she wants to be left alone."

Just then, a couple came over to Tracey, thanked her for a great party and said goodnight. Ten minutes later, two more followed suit. Gradually, the crowd began to thin. People stopped dancing. Nick closed the bar. In about forty-five minutes, everyone had gone.

Nick looked around at the post-party scene. "Johnny and I will get things straightened up out here," he said.

"Oh, thanks, guys, but we have a cleaning crew coming in the morning," Tracey said. "Let's sit on the porch awhile."

"Only for a few minutes and then we'd better go," Nick replied. "I'll go up and say good night to your mother before we leave."

When they decided to leave, Bianca walked to the car with Johnny. At the front door, Nick held Tracey in his arms. "Will you call me tomorrow morning and let me know how your mother is?" he asked.

How many men are as caring as he? she wondered. Overcome with emotion, she could only nod her head.

"If you'd rather not visit with my mother tomorrow night, we can make it some other time," he said.

"It depends," she said. "If Mom's all right tomorrow morning I'll go to work and I'll go and see your mother as planned."

He kissed her. The kiss contained all the tenderness and understanding she knew was part of his nature. With his rare empathy, he was able to match his kisses to her every mood.

In the midst of apprehension and regret, she knew a joy she'd never known before.

Chapter Sixteen

T racey wakened early the next morning and smelled coffee. *Mother must be all right,* she thought. *She'd started breakfast.*

She threw on her robe and hurried down to the kitchen.

"Are you feeling better today, Mom?" she asked.

"I'm fine," Mother replied.

She seemed preoccupied, Tracey thought. She decided not to say anything about the party. The party was what brought on Mother's blue mood in the first place, and that had led to the regrettable decision to tell her the truth.

"Are you working today, Mom?" she asked.

"Of course," Mother replied. "Why not?"

Again, Tracey thought she seemed preoccupied, but there was nothing to indicate she was depressed again.

When Bianca came down for breakfast, Mother greeted her with a smile.

"It's been so nice having you here," she said. "Visit us again."

Tracey decided there was no need for her to stay home from work.

Before she and Bianca drove to the ferry, she called Nick at home and told him Mother was all right and she'd see him that night.

When she got to her office, she phoned home. Mother answered.

"Are you okay, Mom?" she asked.

"I wish you wouldn't keep asking me that," Mother replied. "Just because I had the blues last night and made a fool of myself doesn't mean I'm ready to be hospitalized."

Tracey sighed with relief. She sounded more like herself. Though a sense of preoccupation came through in her voice, this was understandable. She'd had a shock. It would take time for it to wear off.

"I'll see you tonight, Mom," she said. She hesitated before adding, "Nick's taking me over to his house after dinner for a visit with his mother."

"Don't worry about leaving me alone," Mother said. "I have a stack of work. I'll be at the computer all evening."

*   *   *

On the way to Nick's house that evening, worrisome thought began to plague her. What did his mother want to talk to her about?

She glanced at Nick, at the profile of his strong, handsome face, eyes intent on driving the truck through traffic.

Suddenly, she heard him laugh. "I can feel you looking at me."

"I like looking at you," she said.

"Thanks. That's the first thing you've said since we left the hill. I guess you were worrying about your mother."

She wanted to tell him it was *his* mother she'd been worrying about. She felt as though her mind were caught between her mother and his. How she wished she could tell him her concerns about not being Italian nor Catholic. But if she did, she sensed it would bring her closer to the word she was not yet ready for.

The Ferrone's living room looked strangely empty, Tracey thought, as she sat down on the couch. No Aunt Tessie or grandparents or anyone else except Nick and his mother. She must have banished them all to their bedrooms, she decided.

"We'll have coffee and cake later," Mrs. Ferrone said, seating herself in a nearby chair. "For now I want to talk to you, Tracey." She looked at Nick. "Why don't you go and visit with your father?"

Tracey felt a twinge of misgiving. If Mrs. Ferrone

didn't want him to hear what she had to say, it had to be about the ethnic and church difference. She recalled the words that had brought her such joy. *"Our Nick."* Though the antagonism had gone; though her manner had warmed up, was she now going to say she wanted an Italian Catholic girl for Nick?

Mrs. Ferrone waited until Nick left the room before fixing her dark eyes on Tracey. "I want to apologize for acting so unfriendly to you at first," she said.

Tracey didn't know how to reply. She couldn't say she didn't notice. She managed, "It's all right, Mrs. Ferrone."

"When Dominick went out in the storm that night to see if you were all right, I knew he had deep feelings for you," Mrs. Ferrone said. "He told me the street you lived on in Grymes Hill, and I was worried because I knew only rich people could afford to live there."

Tracey stared at her in puzzlement.

"Then when I met you—the day you picked him up for the wedding in your fancy car—I thought you were a snobby rich girl and were probably looking down your nose at our Italian family and plain old house."

Tracey gasped, unable to speak. Could she have said or done something to give Nick's mother this impression?

"Then we all saw the piece in the *Advance* about the multi-millionaire who used to live on Grymes Hill and we noticed his name was Wood, and Dominick said he must be your father. That made me think, all the more, you'd look down on us and Dominick would be making a big mistake if he got serious with you."

Tracey spoke through her overwhelming surprise. "I'm not a snob, Mrs. Ferrone. If I'd ever shown any signs of it, my father would have turned me around in a hurry."

"When you suggested bringing that actress to meet us, I said to Tessie, 'Maybe we were wrong about her. She wouldn't want her friend to meet us if she thought we weren't good enough.' Well, that night I could see you were crazy about Dominick and you wanted his family to like you. It didn't matter that we're only middle-class Italians. Then when that soap opera star started coming on to Dominick, I said to myself you had to be warned. I didn't want her to get him away from you."

"You thought I was a snob? That was the only reason you weren't friendly?" Tracey asked.

"What other reason would there be? Except for that, I would have thought you were the perfect girl for Dominick."

Tracey couldn't keep it in any longer. "I thought you didn't like me because I'm not Italian and I'm not Catholic."

"What?" Mrs. Ferrone gave a hearty laugh. "If I was as narrow minded as all that, my daughter Estelle would be in big trouble. She's marrying a man named David Feinberg."

Nick came into the room at that moment. Mrs. Ferrone rose from her chair. "It's time we had coffee and cake," she said. "You want to help me in the kitchen, Tracey?"

The significance of her talk with Nick's mother didn't strike her until she and Nick were on their way back to Grymes Hill. Then it hit. There were no more reasons to hold back her feelings for Nick. She knew when he was ready to speak the words of commitment, she'd be ready to hear them.

When they got to the house, Mother was in the den at her computer.

"I'm glad you're home early," she said. "I'm almost through here, and then I want to talk to you."

She didn't seem preoccupied anymore, Tracey thought.

Mother shut down the computer and joined them on the couch. "I've decided to sell the Blue Bomb," she said.

As they stared at her, speechless with surprise, she laughed. "I know you've wanted me to do it for a long time, Tracey."

Tracey nodded. "I know I have, Mom, but I didn't think you ever would."

"What made you decide?" Nick asked.

"It was what Tracey told me last night," she replied. "I guess you know all about that, Nick."

"Yes. I take the blame. I kept urging her to tell you."

"I'm not blaming anyone. You both knew it was something I ought to know. I'm thankful you told me, Tracey. I'm thankful to know your father didn't leave because he'd stopped loving me. And though it was a shock to find out the reason behind his leaving I'm thankful to at last know why."

She paused to look at each of them. "I've wasted nine years of my life over something I brought on myself," she said. "I drove away good friends and stopped doing things I used to enjoy, all because of my bitterness. I've done a lot of thinking since last night, and now I know it's time for me to pick up my life. That's why I'm selling the Blue Bomb. It was a symbol of happier days. I don't need that symbol anymore. From now on, I'm going to get back into life and be happy."

"Oh, Mom, you don't know how many times I've prayed for this," Tracey said, throwing her arms around her.

Nick leaned over and gave her a hearty kiss. "Go for it, Christine," he said.

"I'm going to have all my old friends over for dinner as soon as possible, and I'm going to start playing golf again," Mother said. "And I'm going back to my volunteer work at the hospital and will start going to church again."

With a twinkle in her eye and a smile on her face, she added, "but first I'm going out and buy the snappiest little luxury car I can find."

After she'd gone to bed, Tracey and Nick went out to the pool and sat on the kissing bench.

"All's well that ends well," Nick said, gathering her into his arms. "I know how happy you are, because I feel the same way."

"I don't think I've ever been happier," she replied. "But I can't help feeling sorry for the Blue Bomb. It will probably end up in a junkyard."

"Never," Nick said. "We can't let that happen. If it hadn't been for the Blue Bomb, we never would have met."

"Do you think it's possible someone who likes good old cars might buy it and keep it?"

"Sure. You're looking at him."

She kissed him. "You're unbelievable," she said. "Are you sure you're not an angel?"

"I've wondered the same thing about you," he replied. He looked into her eyes. "Only an angel could be aware of my family situation and not be turned off."

"Your family situation?"

He nodded. "Don't tell me you haven't noticed."

"I've noticed how caring you are."

"Not caring enough as far as my mother is concerned. I've allowed her to run herself ragged, taking care of the house and everyone in it, including two invalids and two semi-invalids, and I haven't tried hard enough to put a stop to it. But that's going to change. I'm going to insist that my grandfather goes to a nursing facility specializing in Alzheimer's, and

I'm hiring a full-time male nurse, to take care of my father until he recovers. I've already arranged for a cleaning service to come in twice a week starting next week, and I laid down the law to my two kid sisters about picking up after themselves and doing their own laundry. My mother will put up a fight about all of it, but I'm standing firm."

"I'm glad," she said. "Your mother has been carrying a terrific load."

He tightened his arms around her. "I haven't told you the best part. As soon as things settle down, I'm going to move out."

She looked at him, startled. "Where are you moving?"

"I don't know yet, but I thought maybe you'd help me look around for a nice little house."

Her heart began to race. "Sure, Nick, I'll help you look," she said.

"I'd like it to be in a neighborhood with lots of trees and gardens," he said. "It wouldn't be anything like Grymes Hill, but it would be a good place to start." He looked into her eyes. "I think you know what I'm leading up to, Tracey."

She could only return the look and nod her head.

"That day we met, it was like a big neon sign flashed in my head, with big, bright letters spelling L-O-V-E," he said. "I can't wait any longer to tell you I love you, Tracey. Will you be my wife?"

The day they'd met, there was a sign in *her* head,

too, she thought, but the word wasn't complete. Now, as she whispered "yes" and raised her mouth to his for the kiss of their commitment, she knew the "L" word shone in her eyes, spelled out for him to see.

"I love you, Nick," she said.